Longarm whistled softly...

"You sure must be fond of me, Billy. The last time me and Raining Stars smoked the calumet he wasn't holding captives, male or she-male. He was low on food and ammo. He'd lost a lot of his young men to the Seventh Cav. He was in what you could call a communicative mood. I still sweat bullets riding into his tipi ring alone, and if you think I'm about to do so again, with him on the prod, restocked, with trade ammo, and holding a white gal captive—"

"Damn it," Vail cut in, "if you can't make them South Cheyenne see the error of their ways we'll have another full-scale Indian war on our hands this summer! Is that what you want, Longarm?"

"I never wanted the *last* one..."

D1714535

TABOR EVANS

LONGARM

AT
FORT RENO

A JOVE BOOK

LONGARM AT FORT RENO

A Jove Book/published by arrangement with
the author

PRINTING HISTORY
Jove edition/January 1985

ISBN: 0-515-06274-X

Jove books are published by The Berkley Publishing Group,
200 Madison Avenue, New York, N.Y. 10016. The words
"A JOVE BOOK" and the "J" with sunburst are trademarks
belonging to Jove Publications, Inc.

PRINTED IN THE UNITED STATES OF AMERICA

Chapter 1

Miss Morgana Floyd, the head matron of the Arvada Orphan Asylum, was enjoying the opera immensely. But she would have enjoyed it even more had her escort been less mysterious or at least better looking.

The shapely Morgana had never enjoyed the luxury of a private opera-house box, even wearing her own duds, and she was neither unaware of nor at all displeased by the admiring glances her expensive albeit borrowed red velvet gown and plumed Paris hat attracted when the house lights flared between acts. But every time she leaned forward to see and be seen a mite better, her prissy escort hissed like a stomped horny toad and hauled her back into her plush seat as if he was afraid she'd take the bit in her teeth and dive headfirst into the orchestra pit below, for heaven's sake!

So by the time Carmen had poor Don José in serious trouble, Miss Morgana Floyd was having serious misgivings about the sort of trouble her escort could get a nicer gal than Carmen into.

For openers, when Deputy U. S. Marshal Custis Long had extended her an invite to the opera, of all places, Morgana had of course assumed he meant with *him*, not prissy old Henry, who played the typewriting machine at the marshal's office. And, worse yet, Henry was starting to act downright spooky. So the next time the lights went up she leaned toward him instead of the box rail and said, "Durn it, Henry,

1

if you don't tell me just what's going on here, I'll...I'll scream or something! What am I doing in another woman's opera box, wearing her duds and hat? Where did she and Custis go tonight instead? What are you and your friends trying to pull on me, Henry?"

Henry sighed and said, "I never met the Widow Green before this very evening and I'm not exactly Longarm's friend. We just happen to work for the same boss, and Marshal Billy Vail's sure to fire us both if he ever gets wind of this skullduggery. So please don't lean out over them footlights, Miss Morgana, lest someone notice you ain't exactly the lady as usually sits up here when the opera company's in town!"

Morgana raised a fetching eyebrow in the shade of her big borrowed hat. "So *that's* why the lady Custis introduced me to earlier tonight insisted I borrow her fancy outfit as well as her opera seat, on account, she said, she couldn't make this particular performance! You and that rascal, Custis Long, mean to set up some sort of alibi for that other woman and...Oh, Henry! Tell me *Custis* don't need an alibi for what I fear, knowing Custis, they may be doing at this very minute!"

The prissy clerk blushed beet red and stammered, "I assure you the Widow Green's not that sort of woman, Miss Morgana!" He felt rather proud of himself when he resisted the impulse to add, "Now."

Morgana sniffed and replied, "That may well be. But we both know what a rascal Custis can be, if a girl's not careful."

Henry didn't answer.

So she said, "Well?" and when he answered, "Well what, ma'am?" she scowled as hard as such a pretty young thing could scowl and insisted, "If he's not playing slap and tickle with that other woman, where's he at?"

Henry gasped. "For Pete's sake, keep your voice down,

Miss Morgana! I fear you're attracting attention with that strident tone."

"I'll attract attention indeed!" she warned. "Unless you tell me where Custis and that good-looking widow woman went, and how come!" So, despite Longarm's instructions to the contrary, Henry blurted, "Right about now they should be slickering *another* audience, if they timed it right!"

They had. For as Carmen went on acting mean as hell at the opera house, Longarm was making his own stage entrance at the Denver night court a few blocks away. He was trying to look surprised as well as respectable with his dark brown Stetson freshly blocked and his tobacco tweed suit newly cleaned. He tried to look indignant, too, as he asked the uniformed court bailiff what in thunder the local law might want with a federal deputy at such a time and place.

"Judge Kane is waiting on you in his chambers, Longarm," the bailiff told him. "The boys raided Madam Gould's this evening and caught 'em a sort of confusing situation. Come on, I'll carry you to the private hearing."

Longarm went on looking bemused and innocent as the bailiff led him through the dingy courtroom packed with shabby or flashy-looking folk, depending on what they were doing in night court.

Municipal Judge Kane's private chambers were a mite fancier, with no dirty words or tobacco spit allowed on the mustard plaster walls. The judge was seated behind his desk with Crawford of the *Post* perching the seat of his checkered suit on one corner. An utterly miserable as well as totally confused-looking old gent in a preacher man's outfit sat on a bentwood chair in front of the judge. Across the room a flashily dressed and garishly painted gal of around forty, give or take a hard life, had her rump resting on a cold office stove as she buffed her nails.

3

Despite the heavy makeup on her handsome but sort of hard-looking face, the overhead lamps betrayed a jagged scar down one cheek that all the powder and paint she could get to stick failed to hide.

Longarm looked surprised to see her there, but he ticked his hatbrim to her anyway as he said, "Evening, Leadville Rose. No offense, but I'd heard you'd retired."

The painted woman shrugged. "A girl has to eat, Longarm," she said. "I'm surprised to see *you* here, too. Since when is fornication a federal offense?"

Before Longarm could answer, the unhappy-looking preacher man wailed, "I *never*, you whore of Babylon!" Then he turned to the judge. "She's a raving lunatic, Your Honor! As I told you before, she's one of my parishioners, the Widow Green, and anyone can see she's gone out of her mind! I knew, of course, she was a former harlot, but—"

The reporter, Crawford, cut in with a boyish laugh. "You call her a *former* harlot, Parson Howard? I'd say she was working at her trade with considerable enthusiasm when the copper badges caught you with her in the biggest whorehouse in Denver!"

Crawford winked at Longarm and explained, "He was going down on her when the boys raided Madam Emma Gould tonight. So he may be telling it true when he says he never *screwed* her, the dirty old cuss."

Judge Kane, who looked something like a dirty old cuss himself, snapped, "Don't talk dirty in these here chambers, damn it. The distasteful details of what these two was doing when the house of ill repute was raided ain't as important as the fact they was doing *something* unlawsome according to the Denver municipal ordinances regarding lewd behavior in general and prostitution in particular!"

Longarm shrugged and said, "Don't look at me, Your

4

Honor. I wasn't there and, no offense, Miss Leadville Rose, I'm just as glad I wasn't."

"You're here as a friend of the court," Judge Kane said. "Crawford, here, tells me this woman is the notorious Leadville Rose and that you can back him up on it. So what's it going to be, Longarm?"

The tall deputy smiled sort of sheepishly and replied, "You just heard me call her Leadville Rose and you just heard her answer to the name, Your Honor. I surely want it on the record I only knew her *lawsome* when she was showing more of her charms to the boys up Leadville way that time. I can't say if them rumors about a rose tattoo are true or false."

Judge Kane frowned. "Rose tattoo? What rose tattoo?"

The reporter from the *Post* volunteered, "She's got a big red rose tattooed on one tit, Your Honor. That's why they call her Leadville Rose, see?"

The woman across the room laughed brazenly. *"You* never saw my art collection, newsboy. For I charged more than they were paying you in them days, remember?"

Crawford smiled back at her coldly and replied, "I remember my early reporter days all too well, Rose. We were both a lot younger when you were the top whore of the mining camps. What happened to your face since then, aside from old age, I mean?"

As the woman cursed, or sobbed, and put a hand to her scarred face, Longarm said softly, "Cut it out, Crawford. Aside from being sort of down, she's a she-male as well. So don't kick her no more. I mean it."

Leadville Rose tossed her head defiantly. "I don't need no white knights, Longarm," she said. "Just bring cash. I messed up that other whore's face worse than she messed mine and, if I'm getting a mite shopworn, I'm still a great lay. Just ask the parson, there!"

5

Parson Howard leaped to his feet and sort of did a Kiowa scalp dance around his chair as he cried, "That's a lie, a lie, a lie!" The judge finally yelled for him to sit back down and he did, with Longarm's gentle help.

When they could hear each other again, Judge Kane said, "All right. This fancy gal admits to being Leadville Rose, and two witnesses back her up. So let's drop the nonsense about her being some other gal and get on with this damned hearing. I surely wish you'd plead guilty to being party to an act of prostitution so's I can get back to more serious matters, Parson Howard. It ain't like you're accused of stealing stock or train robbing, you know."

But the preacher man pointed an accusing finger at his fellow prisoner and shouted, "I swear to one and all this is some kind of monstrous trick! I have never been to a house of ill repute in my life, and she is still the Widow Green, of my parish, pretending for some reason to be some kind of painted harlot, and—"

"I thought you said this widow woman *was* a harlot," Longarm cut in, not unkindly.

Crawford asked innocently, "How come the boys arrested you in a whorehouse if you never *go* to such awful places, Parson?"

Howard paled and blustered. "She *is* a harlot. I mean, she used to be, and...Oh, Lord, get me out of this, for only you can tell me how on earth I ever got *into* it!"

Longarm shrugged, turned to the judge, and asked, "Can I go now, Your Honor? I'm a fair hand at chasing stock thieves and train robbers, but I'm not worth a hang when it comes to lunacy hearings."

Before the judge could answer there was a knock on the door and a copper badge Longarm knew as Sergeant Nolan came in. "Your Honor, Madam Emma Gould's sent her lawyer to bail her fancy gal or pay her fine, as the case may be," he told the judge.

6

Judge Kane frowned at the wall clock across the room and asked the male defendant, "How about it, Parson? I could have you home by midnight if you'd be a sport. Just pay the usual fine for unlawsome fornication and we'll say no more about crimes agin' nature, hear?"

Howard wailed, "Plead guilty? Never! I never touched this painted agent of the devil, I tell you!"

Leadville Rose stood up. "Don't be a chump, honey," she said. "They caught us in the act." She shot a world-weary look at the judge and added, "If I plead guilty to plain old whoring and ante up the usual fine, that'll be it, right, ducky?"

Judge Kane grimaced. "I'm not your ducky and it's up to this gentleman if he wants it sweet and simple or not. I warn you both that should this nonsense cost the city of Denver a full jury trial you'd best both commend your souls to Jesus, for your asses will belong to the state prison if *I* have anything to say about it!"

Leadville Rose sauntered over to Parson Howard. "Look, stupid, just plead guilty and I'll pay both our fines. I want *out* of here, you silly old fool!"

Longarm said, "She's right, Parson. You're asking for a heap of trouble, win or lose, in *open court!*"

The reporter from the *Post* frowned. "Don't be a spoil-sport, Longarm," he said. "Let the man *have* his day in court if he wants it. It's hard as hell to fill the front page when the herds ain't in town, damn it!"

That might have done it, had Parson Howard been made of sterner stuff. But when he fainted dead away, Judge Kane told Sergeant Nolan to drag the fool off to the holding tank for now. Nolan said he would, but asked, "What do I tell this fancy gal's lawyer, Your Honor? Does she go or stay for now?"

Judge Kane stared thoughtfully at the painted woman. "I got to study some on that," he said. "She says she's a simple whore with a heart of gold. These other two gents back her up. But that silly rascal on the floor keeps saying she's another gal entire called the Widow Green, and—"

"Oh, shit!" snapped Leadville Rose as she not unproudly opened the front of her bodice to expose her notorious tattoo. "There! Satisfied?"

Judge Kane blushed and said, "Put them tits away, damn it! This is a court of law, not a hootchy-kootchy carnival, and the question afore this court was never whether you had a tattoo or not. Now that I see you do have a big red rose where it ought to be ashamed of itself for blooming, it still don't answer the parson's charge, Leadville Rose, Widow Green, or whoever the hell you might be!"

Sergeant Nolan had been eyeing the woman oddly even before she'd exposed her tattooed but otherwise handsome bosom. He nodded thoughtfully and said, "By gum, Your Honor, this gal *does* look something like the Widow Green, save for that scar and sassy manners!"

Judge Kane blinked hopefully and asked, "Do you *know* this mysterious Widow Green, Sergeant?"

Nolan said, "Not sociable, Your Honor. But I used to see her, some, when I was still pounding that beat up on Capitol Hill. She's a rich old miner's widow. Lives in a fancy brownstone mansion on Lincoln Avenue and drives a matched team of black strutters. I can't rightly say if she's tattooed or not. But last time I seen her she wasn't scarred up like this one."

Crawford snapped his fingers and cut in, "Hell, I know the society gal he's talking of, Your Honor! Scarred or no, she's way too rich to be selling herself at Madam Emma's! She even has her own private box at the opera house and, come to think of it, she's likely there this very minute! You want me to go see, Your Honor?"

Judge Kane sniffed. "Not hardly. Society ladies tend to scream like banshees when someone asks 'em if they knows

8

Emma Gould or anyone who might. I'm beginning to see the light now. This unconscious lunatic on the floor has two gals who look something alike confused in his fool head. Afore he can get us all in trouble with Denver society, we'd best clean this mess up quiet as we can!"

So Leadville Rose paid her bail and was let off for now, while her unconscious co-defendant was hauled to the drunk tank to sleep off his confusion.

Longarm had of course left the courthouse long before the paperwork was finished. He hopped a horse-drawn streetcar up Colfax Avenue to close enough. He didn't want to walk along Lincoln Avenue. He took the alley behind the imposing Lincoln Avenue brownstones instead, and just made it to the rear entrance of the Green residence as Henry and Morgana Floyd drove up to the front of the house, at a clattering trot.

On the surrey seat beside Henry, Morgana was saying, "Goodness, you'd best slow down. It's past bedtime for many folk, this late at night, and you drive as if you mean to wake the dead!"

Henry said, "I know. Longarm said to drive you home at a trot."

"Silly, I don't live *here*. This is the Widow Green's house, and . . . Oh, right, she'll no doubt want her hat and duds back."

Henry reined in, got down to tether the reins to the hitching post out front, and helped Morgana down. Sure enough, lace curtains moved in more than one dark window all about.

Morgana noticed, and she wasn't stupid. As Henry escorted her up to the front door she asked, "Don't you imagine the neighbors are going to talk if we both go in together, Henry?"

Henry sighed. "Not hardly. Longarm said I was to see you to the door and not even kiss your hand. So, now that

9

I've done so, I'd best get out of here while I still have a job!"

Before she could stop him to ask more, the prissy clerk was running back to his hired surrey as if his life depended on it. As Morgana stood there, confused, the door opened behind her and a familiar voice from the darkness inside spoke up. "Come on in. Did you enjoy the opera, Miss Morgana?"

As Longarm closed the door after her she said, "I knew all along that wicked Carmen would come to no good end. But let's talk about this drama *I've* been playing a part in without any idea of the plot!"

He laughed. "Later. First we got to get you out of them duds."

"I beg your pardon!" she gasped.

"No offense, Miss Morgana," Longarm said quickly, "but you're blushing more maidensome than the situation calls for. Your own duds are waiting for you, chaste, in the sewing room. I thought we had it settled that you ain't fixing to seduct me and don't want me to try and seduct you no more."

"I should certainly hope not!"

"Speak for yourself, little darling. But the sewing room's this way and I'm only holding you by the arm, delicate, lest you bust your pretty nose in the dark."

He opened a door. The sewing room was illuminated by a candle. Morgana thanked him, stepped inside, and firmly shut and locked the door in his face.

Longarm smiled wistfully and moved across to the parlor, where a coal fire in the grate shed all the light a man needed to sit down and light a cheroot while he waited for a she-male to get out of one set of duds and into another. He'd just settled comfortably when the door behind him slid open and he turned to say, "That was mighty quick, Miss Morgana."

10

Then he saw it wasn't her and rose to his feet. "That was even quicker, Mrs. Green. Sure nobody saw you coming down the alley?" he asked.

The older woman shook her head. "I felt like a burglar breaking into my own house. But I'm sure nobody saw me. What about the others?"

Longarm said, "If railroad timetables worked as slick they wouldn't need such big waiting rooms. Miss Morgana's in your sewing room, turning back into a pumpkin. Everybody else is where they're supposed to be and we'll be out of here in no time. So why don't you go take that bath you must be hankering for?"

"Don't you think I owe that sweet child an explanation, Custis?"

"Nope. She's likely confused enough as it is, and you surely don't want another lady to see you looking like *that*, no offense."

Felicity Green laughed softly. "You do understand a woman's feelings, don't you? I can't wait to get this garish makeup off."

But she didn't turn to leave just yet. She licked her painted lips and said, "God bless you, Custis Long. I still don't know how you did it, let alone how I'll ever repay you!"

He shrugged. "Go take your bath."

She nodded. "You may find this hard to believe, but I loved David Green very much, Custis."

He nodded soberly and said, "I never doubted that, ma'am. If you're asking do I expect certain favors for services rendered to a lady in trouble, I don't. You reminded me when you come to me for help that your husband and me rode in a war together one time. I told you then that was good enough for a favor or two. So let's say no more about it."

She must have wanted to. She sobbed and insisted, "David told me what sort of comrade you were and that you'd be

11

the one to turn to if we ever needed a miracle. But, Custis, you never knew me at all. Not the *real* me, anyway."

Longarm growled, "Don't go raking up past mistakes, Felicity Green. All I needed to know was that an old army comrade seen fit to marry up with you. I ain't interested in ancient history. So go on and scrub that stuff off, lest Miss Morgana bust in on us to see two grownups blubbering at one another for no good reason. I told you she ain't worldly about mature conversations."

Felicity Green started to say something, choked, and dashed out of Longarm's life, crying fit to bust for some fool reason.

It was just as well. Morgana came in, wearing her own nicely filled but less expensive clothes, to ask if she'd just heard voices in there. Longarm said he was just cussing her for taking so long to dress. Then he led her out the back door and along the alley as he whispered, "We can jaw about it louder in a minute. I'm sorry we couldn't risk Henry leaving the surrey somewhere near. But the streetcars are still running down Colfax, so I'll have you home directly."

She said, "My flat's not too far to walk and it's a lovely night, now that it's dried out from last week's unusual summer rain. I'm not sure I trust you aboard streetcars, Custis. The first time we ever met, as I recall, was aboard the Colfax line, with you shooting it out with bank robbers and me ending up all covered with beer."

He chuckled. "That brewery wagon wasn't supposed to be in the way, Miss Morgana. But all's well as ends well, and here we are on Colfax again, without a streetcar or a brewery wagon in sight."

They turned to walk down the slope toward the less fancy parts of Denver. Morgana's voice was as firm as her grip on his arm as she said, "You won't get away with changing the subject again, Custis. Dang blast it, you *owe* me for . . . whatever it was you got me to do for you tonight."

He chuckled. "I know. The reason I had to keep you and old Henry in the dark was to keep you both out of trouble if my sort of devious play-acting blew up in my fool face."

She insisted, "It didn't. You just allowed we got away with something. So, durn it, *what* did we just get away with?"

As they walked on together he mused aloud, "Let's see how delicately I can put it for your maidenly shell-like ears, Miss Morgana. Mebbe I'd best start her 'Once upon a time.'"

"Custis . . ." she warned.

He nodded and said, "Once upon a time, a few days ago, a lady in distress come to me for help."

"You mean the Widow Green, of course."

"Names ain't important in once-upon-a-time tales, Miss Morgana. Whoever she might have been said she was in an awful fix and that her late husband had saved my hide at Cold Harbor one time. After he done that, he come out West after the War, struck color in the Front Range, met up with her about the same time, and made an honest woman of her."

"What was she before she met up with the lucky prospector, Custis?"

"Don't matter. *His* luck run out when he died of the flux a couple of years back. So she didn't have a man to back her when a loathsome critter crawled out from under a wet rock, claiming to speak for the Lord and, worse yet, doing so from the pulpit of her own church up on the hill."

"Heavens, what did the preacher man accuse the poor woman of?"

"Being less respectable in her wilder youth. He must have felt a mite shy talking dirty in church. So he called on her private, warning her that if she didn't drop out of his congregation he'd say mean things about her from the pulpit. She must enjoy going to church of the Sabbath. For, instead of doing as he ordered, she came to me. He'd given

13

her until this Sunday. Then he meant to haul out all the skeletons of her misspent youth, and . . . Well, suffice it to say we couldn't let him do that."

Morgana frowned and said, "He sounds awfully mean for a man of God. But you still haven't told me what we *did*, Custis. And, by the way, who's *we?*"

He waited until he'd helped her up a high curb and had her aimed right again before he explained. "A man in my line of work gets a chance to do a favor now and again. So once I decided shooting a preacher man out of his own pulpit might be going a mite far, I started calling in debts. A reporter from the *Post* owed me for some scoops I'd given him in the past. Better yet, he was a born practical joker as well as downright poetical when it come to making up stories as we discussed the matter over needled beer. Did you know there's a joke shop down by the Union Depot where you can buy rubber scars and transfers that look just like real tattoos till you wash 'em off again with alcohol?"

"I'm sure you'd know more about alcohol than I do, Custis. But why would you want to look like you were scarred and tattooed? Heavens, everyone in Denver knows you on sight, don't they?"

"Yep. That's why we had to disguise someone not as well known. Another old pal who owed me was a police precinct captain who'd still be pounding a beat had not I shared a couple of arrests with him in the past. Then there was a sergeant on night-court duty who also owes his stripes to me, and—"

"Heavens!" she cut in. "Did you really have to corrupt the whole Denver police force, Custis?"

He grinned and said, "Nope. Just needed a handful of the boys on my side when I discovered it was Madam Emma Gould's turn to be raided this week."

"Oh, Custis!" she cut in again with a gasp. "I hope you're not speaking of the same Emma Gould I've *heard* of! Why,

14

they say she's a veritable white slaver!"

"Emma's gals are more what you could call volunteers, Miss Morgana. Anyhow, knowing she was expecting to be raided, I called in a debt she owed me for helping *her* out one time."

"Hold it! Just what sort of favors would a federal deputy be doing for a notorious . . . *you* know?" she demanded.

He said, "I thought you wanted me to stick to one story at a time. Let's just say old Emma owed me and, better yet, was a good sport about helping out a sort of retired competitor."

"Oh, my God, then the Widow Green was a . . . *you* know, too?"

"I wish you wouldn't keep hollering down conclusions, Miss Morgana. How should *I* know if I was telling the whole truth to Madam Emma or not? The point was that I had to tell her *something* to get her to go along with the joke we was playing on that sassy preacher man, see?"

She didn't argue, so he continued, "I'd meanwhile been checking out the preacher, looking for skeletons in *his* infernal closet. But all I could get on him was that he drank some for a hellfire-and-damnation cuss. He must not have wanted to confuse his parish about his medicinal alcohol. So he drank alone a lot in one of them private velvet-draped booths at the Palace. It so transpired that one of the waiters at the Palace was another old pal of mine. So tonight, when the parson dropped by for his usual snakebite remedy, somebody put some unusual drops in it."

Morgana laughed like a mean little kid and said, "Custis, you're just incredible! First you corrupt the Denver police, then you feed knockout drops to a minister!"

"It didn't hurt him all that much. Just put him to sleep long enough for the boys to smuggle him in the back door of Madam Emma's before they went around to the front to raid the joint. So, when they arrested him doing wicked things to a painted gal and he started talking as crazy as we already knew he was..."

"Wait a minute, Custis. How did they get him to...*you* know...if he was simply knocked out?"

"Now, girl, are you going to argue with what the arresting officers saw him doing with their very own eyes? Or what the fancy gal admitted to the judge they was guilty of? The only question before the court was the mad preacher's charge she was some other gal entire. So, when a mess of us witnessed she was the notorious Leadville Rose instead—"

"Who on earth is Leadville Rose, Custis?"

"Beats me. We just made her up. Though I must say the lady playing the part put on a better act than I expected from any society gal. The judge, aside from the preacher man, was the only one there who didn't know what was going on. It might have been unconstitutional to corrupt a judge, and besides, we wanted it on the court records that the crazy preacher had a nice sedate widow woman confused in his cracked head with someone else, see?"

"I see indeed!" She frowned, adding, "You *used* me, didn't you?"

"Well, you was about the same size and shape, Miss Morgana, and I just couldn't see you playing the part of Leadville Rose. So let's say all I mistreated you to was a night at the opera, free. I thought you said you enjoyed going to operas, ma'am?"

She laughed incredulously. "You big goof. I ought to be angry, but I must allow it's pretty funny. For all save the poor preacher man, at any rate. What happens to *him* now?"

Longarm shrugged and said, "They'll have to let him off when the bailed-out Leadville Rose fails to show up for the trial. The gal in trouble put up the working funds, by the way. The rest of us just enjoyed the joke on a rascal who can likely use a few days in jail to repent his ways. Ain't that your place ahead?"

"Yes. I asked them to leave the porch light on for me," she replied, even as, for some reason, she seemed to want to slow down. "My, it was shorter than I expected, walking downhill. I suppose you'll be going back *up* the hill for your just reward?"

He growled, "Don't talk dirty. Just because we got to acting sort of silly on your sofa that time gives you no call to say things like that. But since you have such an evil mind, I'd best put it on record I don't ever aim to see that widow woman again. It wouldn't help her reputation much to be seen with anyone as cow as me now."

"Thank you for walking me home in public." She sniffed. Then she said, "I'm sorry. You're right. I had no call to be so spiteful about a lady I don't even know. But why *did* you do it, Custis?"

He shrugged and said, "Reckon I'm just a sentimental cuss at heart. When she came to me for help, evoking the name of a long-dead comrade in arms, whoever in thunder *he* might have been..."

Morgana stopped him, turning him to face her under a street lamp as she frowned up at him to ask, "Whoever he might have been? Didn't you just say you rode in the War with her man, Custis?"

He shook his head sheepishly. "Nope. *I* never said it. *She* said it, when she came to me for help. I never met the cuss in my life, in or out of any army. But she had nobody else to turn to, so..."

"Custis, that's just plain crazy, even coming from you! Can't you see she *lied* to you?"

"She didn't lie, Miss Morgana. Her husband just lied to her about his war record. Lots of old boys do that, you know. He may or may not have ridden in the War. He never rode with me. But since I'm sort of famous around town and may have allowed I was at Cold Harbor one time..."

"Never mind *who* lied, durn it!" she cut in. "The point

17

.is that you never owed that woman *anything!* Can't you *see* that, Custis?"

He shook his head. "Nope. I can't. I just told you a lady come to me for *help*. What was I to do, call a dead man a liar and let a mealy-mouthed rascal run her out of her own church?"

They started walking on together again as she said soberly, "A lot of men would have, you know."

He said, "I ain't a lot of men. I'm me. I'm sorry if you think me a fool, Miss Morgana, but I can't help being the way I am any more than you can help being the way you are. So here's your door, I thank you for a lovely evening, and let's say no more about what sort of fool I am."

She murmured, "Maybe the world could use more fools like you, Custis. Would you like to come up for a drink or something?"

He sighed. "I'd like to. Better not. You know how I can get about the *something,* once I've had the drink, Miss Morgana. Like I told you the last time, I *start out* with my mind made up to behave. But after I've set a spell with you on that sofa, smelling your perfume and staring at your . . . eyes . . . Well, I'd best say good night down here, all right?"

Morgana Floyd put her hands on her hips to reply in a determined voice, "No! Are you going to get up them stairs and take your beating like a man, Custis Long, or do I have to drag you kicking and screaming?"

He said soberly, "Don't hit me, ma'am. I'll come quietly."

But later, when they came together, he was sure they woke up the whole neighborhood.

18

Chapter 2

Since they paid him by the day, not by the hour, Longarm had never seen much sense in reporting for work any sooner than a modestly paid federal employee could get away with. But apparently Miss Morgana Floyd was as enthusiastic about her infernal job as she was about sex. For when her big brass alarm clock went off by the bed the conscientious little critter sprang up and was bathed and half dressed before Longarm was even stirring.

Worse yet, for a gal who liked to get on top when the spirit moved her, Morgana displayed iron resolve when he tried to talk her into a fond farewell before she could get her underdrawers on. She said to hold the thought for the coming weekend but that right now she was fixing to be late to work and didn't mean to show up hot and sticky. That part sounded fair to Longarm, but when she reached down and fondled him as they kissed goodbye, he knew he'd never in this world get back to sleep this morning. So as she ran down the stairs to go herd the orphans, he got washed and dressed to see what the hell the Justice Department wanted him to do today.

The federal building wasn't as far from Morgana Floyd's as it was from his furnished digs on the far, unfashionable side of Cherry Creek. So, although he was still the last one in when he got to the office, he was early enough to surprise old Henry some. The prissy clerk looked up from behind his typewriter and said, "My, you sure seem mighty pleased with yourself this morning, Longarm."

"That's only fair, Henry," Longarm said. "You've been looking mighty pleased with yourself since the morning you started working here. Is the boss in the back?"

"Surely you jest. He's in an unusually bad mood this morning, too. You'd best go on in and tell me later about what in the dickens we were up to last night."

As Longarm chuckled and headed for Marshal Billy Vail's inner sanctum, Henry added in a worried tone, "We did get away with it, didn't we?"

Longarm just nodded back as he opened the door to Vail's office and ducked through it. He saw that Henry hadn't lied. The short, pudgy Vail rose from behind his desk and roared, "You son of a bitch! Don't you know this office opens before high noon on a working day?"

Longarm glanced at the banjo clock on the oak-paneled wall, saw it was only a little after nine, and soothed, "Don't get your bowels in an uproar, Billy. It ain't my fault Cherry Creek's in flood and all the bridges are washed out."

Vail said, "Spare me your rustic humor. It ain't all that funny even when I'm in a *good* mood. I'm sending you down to Fort Reno and you just missed the morning train, cuss your lazy hide."

Longarm sat down in the overstuffed leather guest chair near the desk and fished out a cheroot as he replied, "I sure wish you wouldn't do that to me, boss. I'd made sort of important plans for this weekend, and we both know I can't get down to Fort Reno and back that sudden."

Vail nodded. "It's the least I can do for the womenfolk of Denver. You figure to be in the field at least two weeks or more this time. The South Cheyenne has jumped the reservation again. So you got to go down there and do something about it."

Longarm thumbed a match head to light his smoke and didn't answer until he had it going good. Then he blew a thoughtful smoke ring and asked, "How come? We're Justice, not B.I.A. or War. I thought rounding up wayward wards of the government was the chore of Indian agents and such, Billy."

"The B.I.A. requested you personal. Do you recall smoking trade twist with an ornery old Cheyenne called Raining Stars a few summers back?"

Longarm shrugged and said, "Raining Stars ain't ornery for a Cheyenne. After we'd smoked on it some I talked the old rascal into bringing his band in peaceable. I can't see a smart old gent like Raining Stars leading a reservation jump."

Vail grimaced and said, "They say he says nice things about you, too. That's why the B.I.A. hopes you can talk him into acting sensible some more. If you can't, the army means to, less polite. The B.I.A. gets paid by the number of Indians—live ones—they administer to. So it's only natural they frown some on army notions of pacificating Indians. Get the picture?"

Longarm shook his head. "Not hardly. What does the Justice Department get out of chasing Mister Lo? Ain't we got enough *white* owlhoots to chase, Billy?"

"I tried to tell Washington that. But, unfortunately for you, you have a pesky rep as a white man Indians seem to trust for some reason. I know *I* sure as hell can't trust you to turn in a sensible expense account and I've warned you more than once about your odd notions of rough justice. But they still think you might be able to talk Raining Stars into acting sensible. So the next train leaves just this side of sundown, and Henry's already working on your travel orders."

Longarm cursed under his breath. "Before I catch said train, could you give me some hint as to where in the hell I'm headed, Billy?" he asked.

Vail said, "I told you. Fort Reno. That's the South Chey-

21

enne reserve. You got wax in your ears, old son?"

"Not hardly. But Washington must be using shit for brains if they expect me to find reservation jumpers *on* a reservation! How long have Raining Stars and his band been gone, and which direction are we talking about?"

"The B.I.A. ain't sure. They just noticed they was missing a mess of Indians when Raining Stars failed to show up to draw rations for his band last week. They let it go for a spell, figuring he'd forgotten the date or something. Then they sent some Indian police out to Raining Stars' camp to remind him it was ration time. Him and his band wasn't there. It gets worse. A white gal attached to the Indian agency is missing, too. Add it up."

Longarm whistled softly. "You sure must be fond of me, Billy. The last time me and Raining Stars smoked the calumet he wasn't holding captives, male or she-male. He was low on food and ammo. He'd lost a lot of his young men to the Seventh Cav. He was in what you could call a communicative mood. I still sweat bullets riding into his tipi ring alone and, if you think I'm about to do so again, with him on the prod, restocked with trade ammo, and holding a white gal captive—"

"God damn it," Vail cut in, "if you can't make them South Cheyenne see the error of their ways we'll have another full-scale Indian war on our hands this summer! Is that what you want, Longarm?"

"Hell, I never wanted the *last* one. All right, let's say I can talk to the old chief again without going suddenly bald. What sort of deal can I offer him? The B.I.A. has been known to forgive lost sheep, wagging their tails behind them. But even if the white gal they carried off ain't been mistreated, you know as well as me *some* damned fool Indian figures to be jailed for it. And if she's been raped, or says she has, Uncle Sam will feel duty bound to hang more than one of the band."

22

Vail shrugged and said, "You know that. I know that. Let's hope old Raining Stars don't know that." Then Vail leaned back to fold his hands across his overstuffed vest with a weary sigh. "Look, Longarm, I know this is a shit detail they've handed us, but..."

"Not *us*, Billy, *me!*" Longarm said.

Vail nodded and said, "Whatever. I tried to get you off. Why did you think I was in such a bad humor this morning? I wired Washington you'd likely just get your fool self killed. They wired back it made more sense to risk one deputy than a cavalry troop at this stage of the game. So don't look at me like that. It's your own fool fault for getting on so well with Indians, damn it. If you just shot the sons of bitches on sight, like the rest of us, you wouldn't *get* in such fixes. As to this particular fix, you'll naturally pick up some Pawnee scouts and a military escort at Fort Reno. So you won't be going in alone when you catch up with Raining Stars this time."

Longarm snorted in disgust and said, "I won't get near enough to try, tracking him with Pawnee. Didn't nobody ever tell you how fond the Cheyenne are of Pawnee, Billy?"

"They told the B.I.A., too. That's how come you won't have to worry about trusting the Indians on your side. You have to have *some* damned kind of Indians tracking for you in high summer with the prairie gone to straw and the dirt to 'dobe. You'll get more details about your mission once you talk to the Indian agent at Fort Reno. So why are you still sitting there dropping ashes on my infernal rug?"

Longarm rose, but asked, "Do we have any figures at all on the number of braves in Raining Stars' band, Billy?"

Vail rummaged through the papers on his cluttered desk, found the right one, and replied, "B.I.A. makes it around thirty-odd missing Indians all told. Figuring more than half of 'em has to be kids and women, a dozen or so fighting men sounds about right, don't you reckon?"

Longarm frowned thoughtfully and replied, "That's a mighty small war party, Billy."

Vail said, "I know. That's why the B.I.A. wants you to nip it in the bud afore Raining Stars can recruit enough to matter."

Since he had time to plan a more sensible train ride than Henry had typed up for him, Longarm went first to the Union Depot to repair the damages, then rode out to Arvada on a hired livery nag. He found Miss Morgana Floyd alone in her office, as he'd hoped to. After that it was all downhill.

She let him kiss her some, of course, but said, "Honestly, Custis, every time I think I know how crazy you are you just have to prove me wrong! How on earth could I run off to Fort Reno with you this evening? I'm the head matron of this orphan asylum, you idiot!"

He kissed her again and insisted, "I ain't asking you to quit such a swell job, honey. I ain't even asking you to go all the way to Fort Reno with me. I hired us a private train compartment so's we can go all the way just as far as . . . oh, let's say Amarillo. That's where I have to change to the eastbound for Fort Reno. And if you catch the northbound back to Denver you'll make it to work here in the morning only a little later than usual, see?"

She sniffed. "I see indeed! That would mean at least a twelve-hour return trip alone, you beast!"

"Well, you'd have twelve hours of my undivided admiration on the way south, wouldn't you? Look, I ain't asking you to sit up in no coach seat on the way back, honey. I got it fixed with my pals so's you'd get to ride sleeping both ways."

She laughed despite herself and said, "*One* way, you mean. I doubt very much I'd get any sleep on the way south with you!"

He grinned. "I sort of planned to stay awake a lot as far

24

as the panhandle. I thought you might enjoy the ride, too."

She sighed. "You know I would. But I just can't risk it. Thanks to you, I got to work late this morning. Knowing you, and the casual way your chums run their railroad, I just can't take such chances with my job."

He could see he was licked. So he let go of her and said, "Well, at least I get to ride comfortable instead of the way Henry had me set to. I'll try to get back soon as I can. For I'm sure you're prettier by far than anyone I'm likely to meet up with chasing Indians."

She nodded, then shot him a thoughtful look and asked, "Are you still going to keep that private compartment, Custis?"

"Sure. Already made the deal with a pal over to the Burlington Yards. Whether you're coming with me or not, would you expect me to sit up all night just because Henry don't like me all that much?"

"You bastard! I'll bet you mean to find some other woman on that train!"

He laughed easily and replied, "It ain't always that easy on a train going nowhere serious. But if you want to come along and guard your claim . . ."

"Damn it, you know I can't, and damn it, I know *you!* Make sure the door is locked. I'll get the blinds."

He frowned, mildly puzzled, but moved over to lock the barrel bolt on her office door as she'd suggested while, behind him, he heard her draw the blinds, plunging the office into semi-darkness. But as he turned around it was still light enough to admire the view a lot as Miss Morgana Floyd unbuttoned her starched uniform down the front. So he returned the compliment by getting out of his own duds as fast as he could and they were going at it hot and heavy atop her desk when there came a rap on the door and he froze inside her, stockinged feet on the floor.

Morgana's voice was cool, considering, as she called

out, "Yes? What is it?" even as her warm, moist vaginal flesh went on fondly sucking his raging but now confused erection.

A small, shy voice from the other side of the locked door said, "Miss Morgana, Tommy Boyle says I'm too little to play kick the can. Do you think I'm too little to play kick the can, Miss Morgana?"

"Is that Shirley?" Morgana asked, raising her knees to lock her high-button shoes around Longarm's buttocks.

The child answered, "Yes'm. Can I come in?"

Morgana suppressed a moan of pleasure as Longarm, taking the hint, began to move in her again, as quietly as an oversexed mouse. She called out, "Not right now, dear. Miss Morgana is busy. But you can go tell Tommy I said you were big enough to play with him and the others."

Then she couldn't resist whispering up at Longarm, "Oh, Jesus, that's more than big enough to play with *anybody!*"

The orphan outside asked, "Did you say something, Miss Morgana? Can I go now?"

Morgana moaned, "Yes, dear, you can go, and, oh, I'm commmmming!"

Longarm waited until he heard childish footsteps fading away before he groaned, "Hey, wait for me, little darling!" and pounded her to full glory with her soft rump bouncing on the hardwood desk.

As he ejaculated in her, Morgana said, "For God's sake, I hope there's more where that came from, darling!"

But as he proceeded to prove he could do it again, another fool kid pounded on the door, harder, and a whining voice called out, "Miss Morgana, Shirley says we gotta let her play kick the can and she don't play fair, gol durn it!"

Morgana swore under her breath, pushed Longarm off, and sat up to shout, "You just do as I say, Tommy Boyle. Can't you see I'm busy in here?"

"No, ma'am. I can't see nothing, with your door locked.

How come I got to play with sissy old girls, durn it?"

Morgana laughed, sort of wild-eyed, and shouted, "You do as I say, Tommy Boyle. When you're a little older you may find playing with girls isn't all that tedious."

Then, as he, too, went away for the moment, she sighed at Longarm and said, "It's no use, darling. They never give me a minute's peace around here. But at least you won't be in any shape to betray me with another woman on that train tonight, right?"

He told her to perish the thought as he morosely proceeded to put his pants back on. But for a gal who screwed so good, Morgana had a lot to learn about the natural feelings of menfolk. He hadn't even been thinking about any gal save her, up until now. But now that she'd gotten him all hot and horny again, with no chance to finish right, he just couldn't help wondering if that other old gal he knew up on Sherman Avenue would enjoy a free train ride to Texas that night.

Chapter 3

The other woman wasn't home that afternoon, cuss her pretty hide. So Longarm showed up at the depot alone. He checked his saddle, Winchester, and possibles with the baggage smashers and, as he still had some time to kill before his southbound night train left, he went out to the waiting room to see if they had the latest *Police Gazette*. He wasn't sure a man riding alone with a frustrated virile member really should try reading himself to sleep with a magazine filled with sassy pictures of actress gals in tights, but he had to have something to do on the damned train once it got too dark to watch the scenery.

He was approaching the newsstand, perhaps less attentive to the others in the waiting room than he might have been in Dodge or Tombstone, when a familiar voice cried out, "Longarm! Duck!"

He did, crabbing to one side as well. So the first round aimed at his back slammed into the glass case of the newsstand, scattering broken glass and little glass locomotives filled with rainbow candy drops in every direction. Before the hulking denim-clad brute who'd fired could fire again, Longarm had his own gun out and, even lying on his side on the floor tiles, Longarm's aim was better, and his gun was double-action.

So the gent who seemed so mad at him for some reason hit the same tile floor with three of Longarm's slugs in him and didn't even try to reach for the old Navy Colt conversion he'd let go of on the way down. But Patrolman Culhane of the Denver police, who'd shouted the warning just in time, stepped closer with his own gun out, kicked the mysterious stranger's conversion across the tiles, and then kicked the downed man for good measure, growling, "That'll larn you, you son of a bitch!"

Longarm rolled to his own feet. "Don't do that no more, Culhane." Then, as he saw others gathering around, he added, louder, "You folks all move back and stay there, damn it!" Most of them did. He saw, as he joined the copper badge above the fallen desperado, that Crawford from the *Post* and a little blonde gal he had with him didn't think he meant them. He ignored the reporter and the gal as he dropped to one knee by the man he'd just gutshot and said, "Well, pard, if you have much to say about what just happened, you'd best get cracking."

The man who'd tried to backshoot him and lost stared up glassy-eyed and asked, "Is that you, Longarm? I can't see so good. Who put out the station lamps?"

"You did. I know you must have had a good reason for acting so mean just now, pard. I just can't place your handsome face, and I has a tolerable memory for wanted fliers."

"Do you remember the reward posters out on Bucky Lockheed, you bastard?"

Longarm nodded. "Ain't nobody fixing to collect on *that* rascal at this late date, pard. I wasn't allowed to, as a federal agent, neither."

"Then why did you murder him, you son of a bitch?"

"Watch your lingo. Ladies present. I never murdered Bucky Lockheed, old son. I shot him fair and square, from the front, which is a better break than you just offered me. Do you have a name, pard?"

"Yeah, Lockheed. Tim Lockheed. Do I have to draw you a picture?"

"Not hardly. Most folk has relations. That's one of the

things as makes this job so tedious. I'm sorry we had to meet up under such unfriendly circumstances, Tim. Is there anyone you'd like us to get in touch with for you?"

"Go to hell," said the gutshot Lockheed. Then he closed his eyes and just stopped breathing.

Longarm got to his feet and told Culhane, "I reckon he took his own suggestion serious. I know I already owe you. But could you do me another favor, Culhane?"

The copper badge nodded and told him to name it. So Longarm explained, "I have a train to catch. If you'd be good enough to do the paperwork on this rascal, any reward on him is all yours, if it turns out he rode with his brother that time they stopped the U.P. Flier."

Culhane whistled softly. "Jesus, is that the gang yez was speaking of just now? But wait, Longarm. How can I claim the credit when a whole waiting room full of people just saw you, not me, lay him low?"

Longarm said, "That's easy." He waved the *Post* reporter and his blonde companion closer.

Crawford had already been standing close enough to hear it all. He nodded and said, "Right. Culhane, here, shot it out with the rascal as he was attempting to murder a passenger whose name escapes me, since he left on the night train just now. If anyone wants to argue, who are we to believe, a confused witness or the *Denver Post?*"

Longarm agreed Crawford was a swell reporter. Crawford shook on it with him and Culhane, then said, "Longarm, this here young lady is Miss Portia Todd. She's a reporter, too. Or she would be, if the *Post* would only hire her."

The little blonde smiled sadly up at Longarm to explain, "I just came West with a degree in journalism. Alas, they don't seem to feel I have enough experience."

That sounded fair to Longarm, but he was too polite to say so. He just looked at his watch and said, "Well, I wish you luck, Miss Portia. But now I got a train to catch. It's been nice talking to you."

He headed out for the boarding platform as Crawford and Culhane went on sorting out the mess on the waiting room floor for the *Post*'s readership. He noticed the little blonde gal was headed the same way, with him. So he asked her if she was catching the southbound as well.

She said, "Heavens, no. I never ride a train without my travel duster on."

He said, "I noticed your thin summer calico and straw boater, ma'am. But if you don't mean to ride the train, how come we seem to be about to board it together?"

She said, "It's not due to leave for at least ten minutes. Meanwhile, I was wondering if you'd give me an interview."

He frowned. "Ma'am, I know what we just agreed to back there could be considered a mild fib in some quarters. But I sure hope you don't mean to contradict the *Denver Post*. Culhane's a married man who can use any bounty posted on that rascal he just had to gun."

She dimpled up at him and replied, "Don't be silly. I'm trying to get a job with the *Post,* not make an enemy of it. I just want to submit a feature on you, see?"

They'd reached the boarding steps by now. Not knowing what else to do, Longarm helped her up them. He said, "I got me a compartment somewhere on this car. Let's see, now. One A ain't it. Here we are—Two B."

As he opened the door to the small compartment she sort of tittered and said, "Two B or not Two B? That's cute, but I don't see how I can work it into my feature on you."

He said he didn't see how, either, as he tossed his Stetson on the overhead rack and sat down, pointing a polite chin at the green plush seat across from him. She smoothed her calico skirts and took her own seat with a thoughtful glance at the open door. He didn't see why. He'd left it open on purpose, knowing how some gals felt about the company of men they didn't know too well. She placed her straw purse on the seat beside her and took out a little notebook and pencil stub. Then she asked, "Where shall we begin?"

"Begin what, ma'am? Just what are you reporting on, if it ain't what just happened inside?"

"Silly, this isn't reportage. It's to be a space-rates feature on the famous Marshal Longarm, see?"

"Nope. In the first place, I'm only a deputy marshal. In the second, I ain't famous. I ain't sure I want to be, neither. A while back old Ned Buntline caught up with me in the Parthenon and said he wanted to write about me in his Wild West magazine. I told him I'd sue him if he did. I'd already read what he'd written about Jim Hickok, Bill Cody, and such. I sure wouldn't want such silly stuff written about *me*. For I'm just an old boy from West-by-God-Virginia with a job to do as best I can."

"Mr. Crawford says you're one of the most dangerous men in the West."

"I'll get him for that. I ain't dangerous, ma'am. Sometimes I have to teach dangerous men to leave me alone, but you can't call that dangerous, can you?"

"Of course I can, and I mean to. Do you always shoot that same—ah—Peacemaker, Custis?"

"It ain't a Colt 74 single-action I carry, Miss Portia. It's a double-action Colt Model T .44-40. I'd feel silly calling my gun a Peacemaker even if it *was* a 74. As to shooting it, I don't shoot it any more than I have to. I hate to dispute Ned Buntline, but most of the folk they send me after come quiet."

"I suppose they must, if they know what's good for them! Mr. Crawford says you were a hero in the War, too. Which side did you ride for, the blue or the gray?"

He shrugged. "I disremember, ma'am. It was a long time ago, and we was all young and foolish. Don't you reckon you'd best study on getting off now? I just heard the engine toot, up forward."

She shook her blonde head and said, "I'm keeping track of the time and we still have a good five minutes. Is it true you once nearly had a fight with Wild Bill Hickok over Calamity Jane Canary?"

He laughed incredulously. "Ma'am, when and if you ever meet old Calamity, you'll no doubt see what an insulting thing you just said about two grown men! Where in thunder did you hear such tales about poor old Jim and me?"

"I'll say you deny any romantic involvement with the notorious Calamity Jane. Let's get to the showdown you had in Dodge with the Thompson brothers."

"Let's not, ma'am. The Thompson boys are sort of broodsome cusses and they might be able to read. I warned poor old Jim Hickok about the way they was writing him up as some sort of western wonder. But he seemed to get a kick out of it and said he saw no harm in the gullywashers they were spreading all over about him. Then Cock-Eyed Jack McCall took the whole notion serious enough to gun Jim in the back so's *he* could be a gullywasher, too. You just saw, inside, how even a gent with a modest rep can attract unpleasant strangers with his back. So, if it's all the same to you, we'll just leave me less famous and more alive, for now."

She sighed. "If there's one thing I can't stand it's false modesty. But if I promise not to write you up as Denver's answer to Clay Allison, will you at least give me an exclusive on this mission you've been sent on?"

He said, "It ain't much. Just got to go down to Fort Reno and jaw with some old Indian who thinks he's a gullywasher, too. You write it up as another Indian war if you like. But right now we'd best see about getting you off before this train starts up, hear?"

He meant it. So he started to rise. Then the train started

up with a sudden jerk, pitching him headfirst into her surprised lap as the door slammed shut and locked itself. She gasped, "Heavens!" as he, in turn, knelt in the space between the seats with his nose between her thighs.

He thought it only polite to raise his face from her lap as she said, "I don't understand it! This train was supposed to leave on the hour. Not five minutes before!"

He climbed back to his own seat to glance out the window. "Let's see, now. We ought to be stopping at Castle Rock in less than an hour. You can catch a local back from there."

"I should hope so! I'll mess my dress on this smoky old train, even riding two hours! What time does a northbound arrive at this Castle Rock of yours?"

"I don't own Castle Rock, ma'am. As to when you can catch a train back from there, it depends. There's a northbound due to pass this southbound somewhere near Castle Rock. It depends on who gets there first, see?"

"Oh, dear, with my luck I'll surely miss connections. Is there a decent hotel in Castle Rock, Custis?"

He frowned thoughtfully and replied, "I ain't sure there's any kind of hotel there. Last time I spent the night there I was staying with a . . . friends. But let's see, now . . . Oh, I know for a fact there's a swamping big hotel in Colorado Springs. They don't charge as much as a half-baked hotel in Denver, since hardly anybody ever gets off there. Some foreigner built it under the mistaken impression folks would go to all that trouble just to look at Pikes Peak up close."

She looked dubious and asked, "Won't the railroad ticket back cost me as much as a hotel room if I go that far with you?"

He repressed a smile, knowing she hadn't meant that the way it could be taken, and reached inside his frock coat as he said, "You already got a ticket, Miss Portia."

Then he handed her the round trip he'd picked up for

Morgana Floyd in vain. She blinked in surprise as she examined it and asked, "How on earth did you know you'd need an extra fare?"

He said, "A man in my line of work has to plan ahead, ma'am. And so, speaking of planning ahead, let's eat."

"Let's what?"

"If you're getting off at Colorado Springs we got time to go up to the dining car for supper. If we wait until the steward comes through the cars, dinging his fool dinner bell, we'll never get a table in the mad stampede. So let's go now and get a jump on 'em."

Portia seemed impressed when, just as they'd worked their way forward through a dozen cars, the dining-car steward unlocked the door of the rolling beanery from the other side, smiled at them, and said they were just in time. Longarm wasn't as surprised as the little blonde. He'd never seen much sense in packing a watch if a man had no intention of keeping track of the time.

A waiter seated them at a table covered with fresh linen and even fresher locomotive cinders and took their orders. Longarm told her the steak and potatoes was tolerable on this line, but she ordered brook trout instead. He didn't argue. In the crueler overhead light of the dining car he could see she had a modest weight problem she was so far holding to a Mexican standoff by eating sort of sissy. At the moment the softness of her throat and the interesting way she bulged her bodice reminded him more of tempting marshmallow than plain old lard.

Like most folk raised country, Longarm wasn't given much to conversation as he ate. But as she picked at her own supper Portia kept pestering him about his mission and, a morsel at a time, got about as much as he knew about it out of him.

Like most Easterners, she tended to get things about Indians all mixed up even when she'd been told the plain facts. She asked, "Aren't the South Cheyenne the ones who followed Chief Dull Knife on the warpath a year or so ago, Custis?"

He swallowed and replied, "Nope. Dull Knife's band was *North* Cheyenne, and that reservation jump was more an enjoyable outing for the U.S. Cav. than a warpath. Dull Knife wasn't out to lift hair. He just wanted to go home."

He took a sip of coffee before he added, "Can't say I blame him. Had it been up to me, they'd never have put North Cheyenne as far south as the Indian Nation. They ain't used to the dry summer heat and sunburned prairie south of the Arkansas Divide. So it likely spooked 'em. Indians spook at things few white folk understand. But you'd think the B.I.A. would hire at least a few Indian agents who savvy Indians."

"Do *you* understand Indians, Custis?"

He shrugged and said, "I try to. I talk Sign pretty good. Know a few words of the more important lingos. Know better than to argue religion with a man who sees the world a mite different from how I was taught. The South Cheyenne ain't as hard to savvy as some I've swapped shots with now and again. For one thing, they talk an Algonquin dialect, and that's the Indian lingo most of us already have a head start on."

She wrinkled her perky little nose and said, "Speak for yourself, cowboy. I don't know a word of *any* Indian language!"

He said, "Sure you do. Don't you know what is a squaw, a skunk, a pair of moccasins or a bowl of succotash? Them's all pure Algonquin words. You see, the first Indians the Pilgrims met up with spoke Algonquin, so . . ."

"I thought squaw was an insulting term for an Indian woman," she cut in, adding, "I was told in Denver never, never to call a Sioux woman a *squaw!*"

He nodded. "Lakota don't like to be called Sioux, nei-

36

ther. But you're talking about another lingo entire and, like I said, Indians spook over things we might not notice. Most Plains Indians set great store on being proud. So they sometimes carry pride to nitpicking that could be sort of amusing, if they didn't get so *excited* about real or fancied insults. I fear that's what I'll find at the bottom of this latest reservation jump at Fort Reno. I can't think of any sensible reason for Raining Stars to be acting so silly."

She tried some of her own black coffee, made a wry face, but resisted the tempting sugar bowl between them, and suggested, "Mayhaps, like Dull Knife, he just wants to go home?"

Longarm shook his head. "He and his band *are* home. The South Cheyenne lucked out when the army rounded 'em all up and moved 'em to Fort Reno. They'd only been roaming a few miles to the west in the first place. South Cheyenne are used to the summer prairie and cottonwood draws all about the reserve they're supposed to stay put on. So that can't be it."

"Maybe they just can't stand being fenced in like prisoners."

"Shoot, Miss Portia, I can see you've never been on an Indian reserve west of the Big Muddy. Most of 'em are bigger than some whole states back where you come from. There ain't no fences around 'em. They're just big blobs of set-aside, mostly open country. The resident Indians are allowed to wander about all they like. They can even leave the reserve if they tell the agent where they're going and when he can expect 'em back. So, don't think of a reservation jump as a jailbreak. It's more *serious* than that."

She said she didn't understand. So he explained, "Indians out here are classified as Friendlies or Hostiles, depending on how they've been acting recently. If an Indian don't want to fight no more, he makes his mark and gets a government number. Then he moves his wife and kids close enough to

37

his Indian agency so's Uncle Sam can keep an eye on him. Once a month he draws rations and allowance from the B.I.A. Each family gets scrip or cash, depending on how much Uncle Sam trusts his nation, and he's free to buy anything but liquor at the reservation trading post."

"I didn't know that. Even guns and ammunition?"

"Sure. The army and the B.I.A. still argue about that some. But as long as he's classified a Friendly, an Indian is a ward of the government with the same constitutional rights as, say, a white minor. He don't get to vote, and they hope to keep him a Friendly by not letting him get drunk. Otherwise, he lives as good or better than many a white teenager. For one thing, I ain't never heard of a nine-year-old Indian working in a cotton mill or coal mine back East. They don't have to work at all if they don't want to, and most of 'em don't want to. There's worse lives than a reservation Indian's. Ask any cowhand."

"Perhaps. But wouldn't a proud chief like this Raining Stars long for more... well... freedom?"

"Freedom to do what? The south herds have been shot off. So there goes the buffalo hunts, even for us. White men ain't allowed to steal ponies or carry off women these days, neither. Indians can live as close to their old ways as is lawsome, right on their reserve. If an ambitious Indian wants to make more of himself in a changing world, he's free to leave the reserve and take any job he can get, provided he tells the Indian agent he's leaving, so's they can take him off the rolls and such."

She frowned thoughtfully across at him to demand, "Are you saying Raining Stars and his braves were already free to... well... go off and be cowboys or something?"

He said, "Sure. One of the waiters at the Parthenon in Denver is a full-blooded Arapaho. The Diamond K has a couple of Cherokee and at least one Osage rider. I know a whole family of Utes living just down the street from me

in Denver who express considerable contempt for their relations living 'on the blanket,' as they put it. Old John
Redfeather works at a bakery and his wife takes in washing.
Their kids go to public school like everyone else's, and
most of the neighbors take 'em for Mexicans."

She looked almost angry as well as confused. "Then
what's all the *fuss* about?" she asked. "Who *cares* if an old
chief and a dozen braves or so have just decided to wander
off for whatever reason?"

"The relations of the white gal they carried off with 'em,
for openers," he said. "You've missed the point, Miss Portia. We're not talking of one or more South Cheyenne who've
decided to go to work in town. We're talking of an armed
band, dressed feathery, leaving impolite. Aside from this
making the B.I.A. and the army nervous, the Indians themselves could be in danger. The wide-open prairie ain't as
wide and open as it used to be, and there's no telling what
a surprised nester or cowhand might do, should he spy a
band of unreconstructed Cheyenne coming his way in the
company of a likely screaming white captive."

She smiled knowingly and said, "Then I *do* get to report
on an Indian war, after all!"

"I sure hope not," he said ruefully. "Would you like
some dessert? The apple pie is tolerable on this line."

She said something about wanting to slim down and
added that she wanted to write some of this down in the
notebook she'd left behind. So Longarm paid up, left a dime
by each of their empty plates, and escorted her back to his
compartment.

As they got inside, she said, "Heavens, it's too dark to
write." So he thumbed a match head and lit the hanging oil
lamp before sitting down across from her again. She grimaced and said, "Oh, there's soot all over this seat now.
Where's it coming from, with the windows shut?"

"Overhead vents, ma'am. They has to be open in sum-

39

mer. Nothing anyone can do about the engine burning soft coal and running against a south wind." He spotted a light outside and added, "We seem to be coming in to Castle Rock. You want to chance it?"

"Not unless you can promise me a train. By the way, I meant to ask you before, how come the ticket you gave me is good for Amarillo and back?"

He shrugged and said, "Beats me. I just said I might need an extra fare, in case I had to bring back a prisoner or something. Reckon they had to stamp *something* on her, and Amarillo's a pretty name."

The train slowed to a halt with a sigh of vented steam. Portia looked out through the grimy glass and said, "I can't say Castle Rock is a pretty *place!* I don't see anything but a water tower and some cattle pens. Is that it?"

"The saloon's on the other side of the tracks, ma'am," he replied, not mentioning the four whorehouses and jail he knew of for certain. She shook her head and said, "Colorado Springs it is, then. How soon should we arrive there, Custis?"

He grinned crookedly. "We *should* have arrived *here* twenty minutes ago. Colorado Springs is another fifty-odd miles. So figure an hour and a half, Lord willing and the creeks don't rise."

"Doesn't this train go any faster?"

"It's supposed to. But we're still running late. Reckon the storm we had about a week ago has them worried. We're running in line with the foothills of the Front Range and the engineer might be nervous about the trestles across the draws. You just missed a real gullywasher, Miss Portia. It don't storm much in the summer out here, but when it does, it makes up for our mostly tedious blue sky days with fire and salt."

The engineer up ahead tooted his steam whistle and they

moved on without taking on or letting off any passengers, as far as they could tell.

As Longarm admired her pretty little face across from him, a bedbug-sized speck of soot settled on her cheek. He said nothing, hoping she wouldn't notice. But she said, "Oh, Lord, this dress is getting ruined!"

"Well, it does show, some, where your checks are white. This old tweed outfit of mine stands up to travel better. But, to tell the truth, if I wasn't in mixed company, I'd have hung it in the closet by now."

"Good heavens, surely you don't ride trains in the altogether, even alone?"

"Who's likely to look? Besides, I got underwear on, don't you?"

"That, sir, is none of your business!" she blustered. Then, despite herself, she laughed.

He didn't think it was funny. He started to get out a smoke. Then he reconsidered the effects that could have in a stuffy compartment with the windows closed and decided he could wait till she got off. He was sort of looking forward to making up the seats into a bed and smoking naked with the windows open and to hell with the soot. He was mildly puzzled as to why that notion seemed to be giving him a mild erection.

She looked sort of pink and flusterpated, too, as she got out her notebook again and said firmly, "Never mind your odd ideas of train travel. Let's talk about that white girl the Indians have abducted. What's her name, Custis?"

He said, "Don't know yet. The first reports we were wired were mighty sketchy. Suffice it to say, the B.I.A. and especially the army frowns on Indians carrying off white gals of any name or description. That's what all the fuss at the Washita was all about."

She brightened. "Oh, I remember the Washita Massacre!

41

That's when that mean General Custer attacked innocent and defenseless women and children, right?"

"Wrong. People always mix up the Sand Creek Massacre with the Battle of the Washita. Some of the same South Cheyenne were involved in both fights. But they were two different fights, in two different places, for different reasons entirely. Chivington and the Colorado State Militia hit the Cheyenne band of Black Kettle at Sand Creek for no good reason and, sure enough, that one *was* a massacre. But it was years later when Custer and his Gerry Owens cornered the same band under the same chief on the Washita. Black Kettle must have still been sore about Sand Creek. Anyhow, he or at least some of his young men had turned bad. So Custer did what had to be done."

She grimaced. "I heard General Custer was a butcher."

Longarm said, "He was. It ain't smart to send sissies after Plains Indians in the butchering trade themselves. Old George wasn't a general, though, just a brevet colonel. I met him once. Didn't like him. He wasn't an easy man to like. But he was right, at the Washita, just the same."

"Right to slaughter harmless, peaceful Indians?" she sniffed.

"Depends on what you call harmless, Miss Portia," he said. "The casualty list wasn't completely on one side at the Washita. The cavalry lost a dozen or so troopers, likely shot by innocent Cheyenne babies. As to women and children killed in a mighty confusing firefight, Custer's men didn't kill *all* the women in Black Kettle's camp. They got the two white women the Cheyenne were holding out alive. One of 'em is still in an insane asylum back East. The other white gal was made of sterner stuff, or maybe not as pretty, so she got over it in time."

Portia blanched. "Good Lord! That's not the way I read it in the papers back home!" she exclaimed.

"I know. Like I said, Custer was unpopular. Partly with

42

good reason. He was sort of a stuck-up cuss. But, to give the devil his due, the reason some in Washington hated him so was to his credit. Grant's Indian Ring was treating the Indians plain disgusting, and Custer kept writing to the newspapers about it. Nobody could never accuse George Armstrong Custer of being an Indian lover. But as a professional soldier he saw how many of the fights they kept sending him into were the fault of greedy politicians. I've met more than one old army man who's sure Little Bighorn was a setup to get rid of Custer."

"Now that," she said, "is ridiculous! Everyone knows he behaved like a fool in his last fight."

Longarm shrugged and stood up to remove his jacket. "Well, most of the Lakota I've talked to about it like to take full credit for what happened up there in the summer of Seventy-six. But I don't know. I wasn't there. I do know most folk forget that Custer, for all his faults, was *not in command* at Little Bighorn. General Terry *ordered* that ill-advised advance out ahead of the main column, and Terry was not a devoted admirer of his sometimes insufferable subordinate."

He opened the tiny closet and hung his coat up. Then he took off his gun rig and draped it over the clothes hook on the compartment door. She asked why.

He said, "You're right about the soot. But I'll keep my vest and pants on till we get to Colorado Springs if you'll promise to do the same."

She called him a fresh old thing, then laughed and said it was tempting, but added, "I don't think I could trust you not to get forward. Mr. Crawford told me about you and the ladies, Custis."

He sat back down and said soberly, "I disremember him and me ever taking out the same gals, Miss Portia. So I can't see how he'd be in a position to discuss my manners, unless *they* gossiped to him. I know *I* never did."

43

Another glob of soot landed on the open pages of her notebook. She said something most unladylike under her breath. "Maybe if we put that lamp out," she ventured. "I am wearing a full chemise and if you promise not to take it the wrong way . . ."

He shook his head. "I try to avoid making promises I ain't sure I can keep, Miss Portia. No offense, but you're a mighty tempting little gal, even with all your duds on. Besides, we'll be stopping at Colorado Springs pretty soon and I don't like to start chores I haven't time to finish, neither."

"Heavens, Custis Long, are you trying to seduce me?"

"No, ma'am. I'm doing my level best to avoid it. Let's talk about the Indians some more."

She giggled and got to her feet to trim the lamp herself, plunging the compartment into darkness, but not total darkness. For there was just enough moonlight coming through the grimy glass to reveal that her underwear was white as she shucked her outer calicos and moved gracefully to the closet to hang them up. He tried not to laugh as he saw she still had the straw boater pinned atop her blonde curls.

Portia shut the closet and started to resume her own seat. Then the train suddenly slowed and she wound up face down across Longarm's startled lap. He looked down at her ample but thinly clad bottom, in perfect position for a good spanking, but decided he'd better not. She gasped, "What happened? How did I get into this ridiculous position?"

He said, "You don't look all that ridiculous to me, ma'am. As to how, we seem to be pulling into Colorado Springs. So the next move is up to you."

He expected her to leap up for her duds, but she didn't move at all. She just lay there across his lap, as if she was studying the situation as hard as him. Then she asked softly, "Didn't you say my ticket was good for a round trip to Texas and back, Custis?"

44

"Honey, you can go as far as you like with me," he said.

Then, as she only answered with another giggle, he got a firm grip on her tempting rump so she wouldn't roll off his lap as he turned her over for a good old-fashioned kiss. The next thing he knew, they were acting depraved as hell. But he didn't actually get it in her until the train was pulling out of Colorado Springs and, when he did, she said he was a beast to take advantage of her like this on an itchy plush seat.

He made her come that way, anyhow, knowing how silly some gals could act if a man was fool enough to take it out before they'd stopped complaining and started pumping back. But once he'd made friends with her, with her high-buttons locked across the nape of his neck and her plump bare hips rubbed red on the plush, she didn't object when he suggested they get out of all those fool duds and between smooth sheets.

As he made the bed up for them, she sighed, "Oh, the things a reporter must do to get a story." But you could tell she was just funning, from the way she stripped entire and dove into the bed ahead of him, whimpering for him to hurry.

Even Portia had to allow it was much nicer bare-ass aboard clean linen as the train tracks clickety-clacked under her in time with her thrusting hips. They went deliciously crazy together for a spell and, for a gal who usually talked so much, old Portia confined her conversation to suggestions about new positions, spoken low and dirty, when it was time to let their fevered flesh do most of the talking for them both.

But habits are hard to break. So once they'd come enough to stop for his second wind and a smoke, Portia said, "I suppose you'll think me a big fibber, but what just happened did come as a total surprise to me, darling. I'm not about to tell a man of your experience I was a blushing virgin.

45

But, heavens, how did we wind up in bed so *soon?*"

"Well, I've always figured the sooner the better, with a cold gray dawn just down the line. Do you really have to go right back to Denver?"

"Why, Custis, what a sweet thing to say? Alas, I can't go on with you all the way. All the way to Fort Reno, I mean. But we might as well go all the ways we can while we still have the chance."

They hardly got a wink of sleep that night, all the way to Texas.

Chapter 4

Longarm had less luck, or perhaps a well-deserved rest, getting the rest of the way to Fort Reno. Nothing he saw getting off the train inspired him to sexual or any other kind of desire. Fort Reno was more a state of mind than a place one could pin down on the real world instead of a map. All of it looked uninteresting.

The railroad had built a jerkwater stop along its right-of-way. This had naturally attracted the usual whores, gamblers, and such ramshackle housing as they required, including an imposing and no doubt handy courthouse and jail.

The army, in its infinite wisdom, had built the military garrison of Fort Reno at an inconvenient distance, so the enlisted men could walk, while the officers rode, far enough that they had a chance of getting back to the post semi-sober. The Fort Reno Indian Agency was even farther out of the so-called town. Hence Longarm decided he needed a drink and a horse, in that order.

The saloon nearest the railroad depot was crowded with cowboys and Indians. It was against the law for Indians to drink, but Longarm hadn't come all this way to enforce that particular federal regulation. He found a space at the bar and bellied up between a white kid who didn't look old enough to shave, let alone drink, and a moon-faced Indian of about forty, dressed in blue denim and sporting an Indian police badge.

Longarm asked the fat white barkeep if they had Maryland rye and the barkeep told him not to be ridiculous. So he ordered a needled beer instead. The Indian policeman said he'd have the same. The barkeep nodded but said, "You ain't an *Indian,* are you? No offense, but I'm supposed to ask."

The Indian growled, "Can't you see I'm a Mexican? *Como esta!*"

The barkeep said that was good enough for him.

As he slid their steins across the mahogany at them the white boy to Longarm's left suddenly keeled over backwards to the sawdust and just lay there, grinning owlishly up at the pressed tin ceiling. The Indian grimaced. "They shouldn't serve drinks to white boys," he said. "Anyone can tell you it brings out the savage in 'em."

Longarm chuckled. "I've noticed that. I answer to Custis Long and I ride for the Justice Department. That badge says you're a B.I.A. lawman and I don't care if you talk Spanish or not."

The Indian said, "I'm Charlie Whitepony and I don't give a shit one way or the other about you, unless you want to discuss my drinking habits."

"I don't," Longarm said. "That kid on the floor there just established the fact that some men can hold their redeye and some men can't. I'm down here about Raining Stars and whatever the hell he's up to, drunk or sober. I'd sure like to hear what you Indian police have to say about it."

Whitepony asked, "How do you know you can trust my word? When I'm not...ah...Mexican, I'm South Cheyenne, like old Raining Stars."

"I figured I recognized the beadwork on your hatband, Whitepony. You'll have to tell me if you can be trusted or not. Since I don't know you, I'll likely have to take your word for it."

The Cheyenne officer stared impassively at Longarm for

a time before he replied, "I never lie. I am a member of the Crooked Lance Society, and we are not allowed to lie. But some Americans are not as trusting as you. Hear me: the army is trailing Raining Stars with fucking *Pawnee!* Hear me: Pawnee can't steal chickens without getting caught, yet they have them trailing South Cheyenne across their own ground. Have you ever heard such nonsense, even from the army?"

Longarm nodded and said, "Yep. They had me scouting with Crow against Lakota one time. They likely figured Crow, being enemies of the Lakota, were less likely to overlook sign."

"That's different. Crow at least used to be part of the Lakota Nation. Pawnee are all assholes. But you are right about the army not trusting Cheyenne to scout Cheyenne. The army has no feelings. They are always insulting us. Hear me: why would I be wearing this badge if I was on the warpath against you people? Do you see *me* riding with Raining Stars? Did *I* kill those white men over to the west? Listen, white man. When I kill white men, I take *hair!* Were those white men scalped? Of course not. But they insult us by riding after our brothers with Pawnee!"

Longarm said, "Hold it, Whitepony. You're getting ahead of me. What white men killed by Indians are we speaking of? There was nothing about that in the wire the B.I.A. sent us."

The Indian shrugged. "The army just found them. Texas trail herders, from the sign those stupid Pawnee say they read. They were camped in a draw when someone jumped them good. Their herd was scattered, maybe a few cows butchered for food. The whites were scattered good, too. All along the draw, as if they put up a good running gunfight. The flies and coyotes found them long before the army did. So who's to say whether all the mutilation was the work of human hands? What I don't understand is that most of them still had their *hair*. But maybe Raining Stars was in a hurry."

"How do they know it was even an Indian attack? White cattle thieves have been known to jump a night camp, too, you know."

"I think you must have a good heart. You are the first American who's said anything like that. But I don't see how it could have been white cattle thieves. For one thing, nobody took their herd. It was still grazing all around, most of it, when the army found the dead drovers. The white men were killed Indian style. They were clubbed to death, not shot. You know, of course, it's a bigger coup to strike an enemy down with a war club than to shoot him?"

"I noticed as much, fighting Lakota a few years back. Come to think on it, I might have met up with some North Cheyenne riding with 'em. You boys are pretty good with them rock and rawhide war clubs."

"Thank you. We try our best. By the way, have you ever fought my people, the *South* Cheyenne?"

"Hell, yes. Hasn't everybody?"

Whitepony smiled for the first time and said, "I'm glad we met after I turned Mexican. You're a *big* bastard. But had we met in the Shining Times I think we might have had a good fight. Now we seem to be on the same side. Or we would be, if the army wasn't so insulting. I think we are both wasting time talking about Raining Stars. By now it should be all over."

"Oh? You reckon the army's caught up with the runaway band, even with Pawnee scouts?"

Whitepony shrugged and asked bitterly, "Where could they go, now? Up the Washita? It's all fenced in and settled by your people. West, to the Arapaho country? What would they find when they got there? More cattle spreads and homesteads. What is there to eat on the sea of grass these days but white men's cows? Why hunt cows when the B.I.A. gives us beef here free? You know what I think? I think

Raining Stars had a vision, a bad vision that's driven him crazy. Even before he jumped the reservation he was old and acting crazy. I thought he was too sick to ride. I thought he would never see another summer. But maybe that's it. Maybe he just wants to die out on the open prairie, away from Americans who laugh at old, sick Indians!"

Longarm finished his drink and ordered two more as he said, "That don't explain his taking along at least a dozen younger men and their women, including at least one white woman. What can you tell me about *her,* by the way?"

The Indian shrugged. "I don't know her. I saw her around the agency from time to time. But she was too stuck-up to talk to Indians. She was the wife of a junior agent. He's been weeping and cursing like a whipped dog ever since Raining Stars carried her off. I don't know why Raining Stars carried her off. He's old and she's ugly. But who can say what an old man's visions might tell him to do?"

"Would the chief put up with it if a younger man decided to carry along a white gal, Charlie?"

"I don't think so. Not a chief with any control over his young men. Jumping the reservation is serious business. Kidnapping white women is more so. Raining Stars is no fool, when he's in his right mind. He'd know that while the army would just bring him back for reservation jumping, they'll have to hang somebody for the silly business with the white woman."

Longarm nodded. "I see we both know how the Great White Father thinks, Charlie. I ain't sure what in thunder *I'm* supposed to do about it at this late date. Who's in charge out at the agency now, if the agent who's missing his woman is so helpless?"

Whitepony took a sip of needled beer with a nod of thanks and said, "Our boss agent is John Miles again this summer. He is not a bad agent. The one he left in charge over the winter was only stupid, not bad. His name is Hutchins. He's

51

the one whose woman was carried off. Even before that happened he was a weakling. Now he is not even a real woman."

Longarm said, "I know old Johnny Miles. You're right. He's a good man, and I can prove it. I had to investigate him one time when the B.I.A. was reformed by President Hayes. But you say this *Hutchins* gent has been in charge a spell? He don't ring no bells at all in my fool head."

The Indian shrugged. "He's new. Now he'll probably go back East and stay there, where he belongs. Miles just placed him in charge for a few months because he had to go back to Washington and testify about Indian beef and other disgraceful matters. Now that Miles is back, things should get better."

"I'm sure they will, knowing Johnny Miles. But let's get back to that temporary junior agent left to mind the store in his absence. Did your folks have any particular complaints against him? Mistreating government wards is as good a way as I know to make 'em jump the reservation."

Whitepony thought, shook his head and said in a grudging tone. "He's a weakling, I'm sure. But he did nothing to make any of my people angry at him. I would know if anyone had been cheated on their rations or allowance. They always send us to lock up angry Indians. As a matter of fact, I think some of my people took advantage of the poor weakling and his stuck-up woman. You know how easy it is to play jokes on the greenhorns. If anything, some of the women got more flour and coffee and clothes for children they might not really have than they would have with the regular agent here."

"Any complaints about the trading post out to the agency?"

"Of course. They always sell us shit nobody else wants. But nobody rode off with the *trader's* woman. Nobody did anything bad to the schoolteacher or the medical staff, either. I think Raining Stars must have just gone crazy. He

52

had no reason to hurt the poor dumb agent in charge and, as I said, the agent's woman was ugly. Too tall. Too skinny. Hair the color of dishwater and eyes as gray as raw oysters. Who would want to steal a woman like that, even if she wasn't stuck-up?"

"What if some of the *squaws* in the band of Raining Stars had it in for the white gal, Charlie?"

"Jesus, I thought you understood our ways. Since when do women tell men what to do? If a Cheyenne's woman wants to fight with another woman, he just tells her to go ahead. He doesn't do it for her. Besides, it never happens between your women and ours. Your women think they are better than our women. Our women know better. So why fight? I tell you, old Raining Stars had a vision. It must have been a strong one. Stronger than the one that gave him his name. And the night the stars fell was powerful medicine!"

"Are we talking about the big meteor shower back in the Thirties, Charlie?"

"You people can call it what you like. We know it was the night the stars fell out of the sky like rain. Raining Stars was out on a hilltop that night, seeking a vision for his true name. As he prayed for the vision, the stars began to rain all around him. One fell near him. And hear me: when he went to it, expecting to find a hot fallen star, he says the star was covered with *ice!* Even as he watched, frost crystals formed on it. I think that must have been *big* medicine! I don't understand what he could have seen more recently that was more powerful, but whatever it was, it drove him crazy. He took his young men out. He carried away a white woman. He killed the first white men he came across in the prairie—with honor, not bullets. I wish *I* could see a vision like that at least once before I go to the Old Woman's Lodge!"

Longarm allowed the old chief must have seen a good

one. Then he asked which of the two livery stables he'd noticed on his way to the saloon hired out the best horseflesh, adding, "As long as I'm here, I may as well say howdy to old Johnny Miles."

The Indian shook his head and said, "Both liveries keep crowbait even a Pawnee would be ashamed to ride. You can get a decent mount out at my agency, though."

"That may well be, Charlie, but to borrow a government-owned Indian pony I got to get *to* it, and I'd rather ride *anything* than walk that far!"

Whitepony called out in Cheyenne, then switched back to English to say, "We can do better than that for you," as a younger, hawk-faced Indian policeman joined them. Whitepony introduced him as Officer Wetfeather and talked to his sidekick some more in Cheyenne before explaining, "Wetfeather can give you and your possibles a lift out to the reserve in our buckboard."

Longarm had already followed at least the drift of their conversation, so he knew Whitepony hadn't asked at all politely. He smiled uncertainly at the younger Indian. "I wouldn't want to be a bother to you, pard," he told him.

Wetfeather shrugged. "Let's go. The sooner I carry you out the sooner I can get back. I have to keep an eye on this old Crooked Lancer. He gets mean as hell when he's drunk."

Whitepony laughed and Wetfeather led Longarm outside, saying, "Buckboard's down the street in front of the skating rink."

"Skating rink, in high summer?"

"Summer skates—on rollers. Ice pond's made of hardwood. You white people do everything crazy. Let's go."

As they followed the shaded plank walks back toward the depot and a big building Longarm had taken for a barn up until now, Longarm said, "Hold on. I see a Western Union sign ahead as well. I'd best wire my home office I got here and ask permission to head right back. It'll only take a minute."

It took more like five. Longarm asked the Western Union clerk if there were any messages for him, found out there weren't, and wrote a day-rates wire to Billy Vail, pointing out that his mission now seemed pointless. The Western Union clerk read it back to him, so Wetfeather heard and, as they went outside and across the dusty street to his buckboard, he asked, "Don't you mean to hunt down Raining Stars after all?"

Longarm shrugged. "Don't see much sense in even trying, now that he's declared open war. The B.I.A. was sort of hoping I could talk some sense into him *before* he started killing whites. Now that he's gone and done it, I can't think of a thing I could say to him that a troop of cavalry couldn't say somewhat safer."

They untethered the buckboard team and climbed aboard. Wetfeather asked Longarm where his possibles were. Longarm said, "Baggage room at the depot. Figured on checking out my saddle and such once I knew where I'd be staying. Don't figure to be staying now, so what the hell."

Wetfeather said that sounded reasonable and wheeled the team to head on out. It didn't take long to get out of town, such as it was. The open countryside between the railroad and the Cheyenne agency rolled more than the prairie east of Denver. The drainage was still running west to east, but the Ozarks over the horizon to the east complicated things and the draws had to wriggle some to keep going. The rises were, of course, summer-dried and overgrazed. Some draws supported crack willow and cottonwood, or would have, had the trees been allowed to grow up. Any trunks more than six inches thick had been lopped for firewood and, since both willow and cottonwood sprouted from the stump, the draws were more brush-filled than wooded.

Wetfeather had been thinking while Longarm admired the scenery. He said, "Your name is Long. You say you know Raining Stars. Raining Stars does not know many of your kind well enough to like them. But my uncle, who rode against you people in the Great Buffalo War, says that once, when he followed Raining Stars on the warpath, their party was cornered, low on ammunition, ready to sing their death songs, when a tall American rode into their camp alone. They called him Longarm. Could that have been you?"

Longarm shrugged and replied, "We was all young and foolish then. I was scouting for the army, just after I come West after the war between the blue and the gray."

"You must have still enjoyed excitement. What made you ride into a war camp of Crooked Lancers alone like that? Did you have a vision?"

"Sort of. I pictured more blood on the ground than the situation really called for. So I came in to explain said situation to Raining Stars and, as I'd hoped, he turned out to be a sensible cuss, once he got through bragging about all the awful things he was about to do to the entire U. S. Army with less than thirty braves and even fewer bullets. I was just doing my job."

"Hear me: my uncle says you did a good thing for both sides. My uncle says you gave your word nobody would have to hang if the band came in with you. My uncle says that when the soldiers waiting over the horizon like women tried to disarm and humiliate the band, you told an officer not to be silly. My uncle says you let them in like men, carrying their guns, proudly."

"Well, the guns were empty, and we'd smoked on it being peace with honor. I've never enjoyed kicking a man when he's down. So I don't do it if it can be avoided."

"Hear me: a lot of your kind do not see things as you do, friend Longarm. I think you should stay. I think you

56

should track down Raining Stars and make him smoke the calumet again. If the army catches him and his band, they will hang them all this time."

Longarm shrugged and said, "When you're right you're right, Wetfeather. But Raining Stars has used up all his second chances with the Great White Father. You folks are allowed to make your mark on a peace treaty once, or maybe even three times. But old Raining Stars has smoked the calumet so often it's sort of ruined his health. A war chief can go from a Hostile to a Pacified on the books. But when he tries to go the other way, he ain't classified as a Hostile again. He's considered a Renegade. We sign peace treaties with Hostiles. We *hang* Renegades. them's the rules. I didn't make 'em up."

"Would you hang Raining Stars if you got to him first?"

"Not personally. But I couldn't stop the government from doing it once I brought him in. Not now that he's spilled more white blood. That's why I aim to head on home as soon as they give me permission. I hate to see anyone hang—and, no offense, you Indians seem to take it even more personally than most."

Wetfeather sighed and said, "A man is allowed to cry when he is being killed in a manner not covered by custom. I hope they took enough ammunition with them to die like men when the army catches them. The agency is just over the next rise."

As he'd said that, they'd just topped another rise, with a brushy tangle of new growth firewood between them and the far slope. As Wetfeather started to say something else, the back of the buckboard seat exploded between them in a puff of hickory splinters. So they were both rolling out on opposite sides when the rifle's report caught up with its bullet.

Longarm landed on one shoulder and somersaulted down the grassy far side of the rise to wind up prone, facing back

57

the way they'd come, with his .44 trained on the empty skyline above. He held it in both hands, elbows braced, and still cursed himself for having left his Winchester behind. Nobody popped over the rise with that more serious weapon they'd just heard. So Longarm glanced to his right to see how the buckboard and its Indian driver had made out.

The buckboard was long gone. The spooked team had naturally bolted when Wetfeather let go of the reins. By now they should be halfway home to the agency. Wetfeather was on his gut in the grass across the wagon trace, his own hogleg .36 aimed the same way as Longarm's .44. The Indian caught his fellow lawman's eye and signaled his intent to circle to the west. Longarm nodded and started crawling up the slope to the east. So by the time the bush-whacker's two intended victims made it to the top they were a good fifty yards apart and should have had anyone on the far side in a tolerable crossfire when they made their final move.

Wetfeather signaled in Great Plains Sign that he was ready to go for broke. Longarm signaled similar intent, then gathered his knees under him and fluttered his free hand against his open mouth in a silent war whoop. They both charged over the rise as one, guns trained on the wagon trace.

But all there was to see was an empty draw, with a faint haze of dust hanging against the blue sky between them and town. Wetfeather dropped to the sod and placed an ear to the ground. Then he stood up again and walked toward Longarm, who met him on the wagon trace between them. Wetfeather said, "One pony. Iron-shod. Ridden by a cow-ard."

Longarm nodded thoughtfully. "He must have been. He had us good with that high-powered rifle. Could you tell which way he rode?"

"No. Only that he was riding away. The ground does

not carry the direction of a coward's flight, only whether he is coming or going. You want to scout for sign?"

"This close to town, on heavy grazed range?"

"I know. I was just being polite. Let's go. I want to beat the shit out of that team when we find them at the agency. Please don't tell Whitepony about this. He has an odd sense of humor and I promised him you would not have to walk."

Longarm holstered his gun with a chuckle, took out two cheroots, and said, "Well, hell, you rode me *most* of the way." He struck a match to light both their smokes before he added, "I fear we're going to have to at least mention what happened to Whitepony, pard. He'd be in a better position than us to say if anyone mean and sneaky-looking rode out of town just after we did. Do you have any particular enemies who might have been bending the liquor regulations back there? I have a reason for asking."

As they started walking, Wetfeather said, "Lots of people resent Indian police. Very few of them shoot at us. The last one who tried to kill me died over a year ago. I thought that bullet was meant for *your* back."

"It could have been. Come as close to hitting me as you. But I just got here. Ain't had time to talk to hardly nobody, let alone make friends or enemies in Fort Reno."

Wetfeather shrugged. "We are both lawmen. We have both had to arrest many people. Maybe next time the coward will take better aim. Then at least one of us will know who he was after."

"Are you always this cheerful, old son?" Longarm asked.

"In our business a man has to face facts."

Chapter 5

The Fort Reno Indian Agency, as usual, consisted of a small, neat compound of white frame buildings surrounded by a shantytown of unpainted frame shacks deemed suitable for Indian occupancy. The Indians could have all the free whitewash they wanted, of course. But, of course, they didn't want it. It was an established fact of the High Plains culture that wood didn't need to be painted unless it was to give it medicine, and that white paint, whatever the Great White Father thought, was the color of death.

More than one Indian agent had talked himself blue in the face pointing out that Plains Indians considered white a *lucky* color, for a buffalo robe or a deerskin wedding dress. But the Indians didn't know how to explain the difference between natural and painted colors. So they just ignored the free whitewash and unpainted Indian housing was the sign of an agency run by an understanding agent.

John D. Miles was one of the best. He came out on his porch as Longarm and Wetfeather approached, nodded to Longarm, and spoke Cheyenne to Wetfeather. Wetfeather nodded at Longarm, too, and went off to track down his runaway team. As soon as the two white men were alone Miles said, "You understand why I had to greet you in the local lingo, right?"

Longarm nodded and said, "Sure. That's how come you kept your hair when Dull Knife got all broody a year or so ago. What did Raining Stars have to say before he jumped, Johnny?"

"Come on inside and I'll coffee you some, Longarm. I wasn't here when poor old Raining Stars went loco. Can't get any of the others to tell me what he was riled about, even in their own lingo. You hear about the killings since?"

Longarm nodded and followed the agent silently inside. Miles waved him to a seat made of rawhide and elk horns. It was more comfortable than it looked. As the agent stepped out in the hall to holler towards the kitchen, Longarm noted the living-room walls were covered with other sporting trophies, framed photographs of various B.I.A. men and important-looking Indians, but innocent of any Indian handicraft. He nodded with approval. Lots of whites living among Indians tended to clutter up their quarters with quaint Indian relics, not knowing how dangerous this could be. Some Texans had been known to wreck a saloon displaying captured Confederate flags.

Miles came back and took a seat across the cold hearth from Longarm, saying, "Coffee and cake's on its way. My wife's still back East and it's hell to get an Osage gal to move."

Longarm raised a thoughtful eyebrow and asked, "You got an Osage cook, Johnny?"

Miles said, "Have to. Can't show favoritism or insult to a South Cheyenne squaw. They take housekeeping for a white family either way, depending. The gal's a runaway from the Osage strip. We took her in when she got this far, heading God knows where."

"How come she run away from the Osage Nation?"

"She don't say. But she's a willing worker, gets along with my wife, and keeps to herself, so what the hell. You reckon you can track Raining Stars? Army sure ain't had much luck so far."

Longarm shrugged. "I tracked him down once before.

61

But do you reckon there's any point in me trying again, now that they've counted coup?"

Miles grimaced. "Not hardly. You ain't an army scout no more and even if you was, you wouldn't be able to make a deal with the band this time. I never would have thought it of old Raining Stars. But he's just turned bad on us. Had a dog like that once. Hated to shoot him. But what can you do when an old hound starts snapping unexpected?"

Before Longarm could answer the coffee and cake came in, carried by a mighty handsome squaw dressed white and, judging from her blue eyes, part white herself. Miles introduced her as Miss Funny Eyes. It didn't surprise Longarm much. Funny Eyes put the tray on a little rosewood table between them and crawfished out, looking sort of spooked, or perhaps her eyes just looked odd and unreadable peering out of her diamond-shaped Osage skull. She made good coffee and tolerable pound cake, though.

As they went to work on the food, Miles brought Longarm a little more up-to-date on the confusion before either of them had arrived. The white gal they'd carried off had been named Helen, and her thoroughbred riding horse had been carried off as well. That didn't help a hell of a lot. But as long as he was here, Longarm knew Billy Vail would expect a full report. He cut in now and again to roll over an occasional rock and see if anything interesting crawled out from under it.

Miles said the deputy was nitpicking. He shook his head wearily and said, "Damn it, Longarm, I've told this same story so many times it's getting tedious. I wasn't here when Raining Stars run off, so I have no notion why. I can't tell you the exactful date because nobody *knows* just when they jumped. Or, if they do, they won't tell any white man. All I can say for sure is that poor young Hutchins missed his wife one evening, wasted time looking for her in town and such, and then, when he had sense enough to ask the Indian

62

police to track her, they noticed Raining Stars and about thirty others was missing, too. The reason it wasn't noticed right off was because the old man lived out on the range a piece. Him and his band kept house in a tipi ring over to Cottontail Draw. I don't think he saw the advantages of civilized cabins. They even *wintered* in them smoky old canvas-patched tents. Come in once a month to draw their rations and allowances, of course. Ain't it odd how even noble savages like paper money better than wampum?"

"Yeah. Red Cloud demanded cash, not shells, for the Black Hills. You issue real money, not scrip, here?"

"Have to, since Hayes took office. You know how the old Indian Ring under Grant played games with agency scrip. You ought to. I was one of the agents you investigated that time. Naturally, you'll want to go over our books afore you leave, right?"

Longarm smiled sheepishly and said, "Not if *you* say they're in order, Johnny. The advantages of my sometimes being nosy in the past is that once I've had my nose far enough into a gent's business I hardly ever need to sniff him again. Of course, records kept by your assistant while you were away..."

Miles shook his head and cut in to say, "Already been over the records kept by poor young Hutchins. He may be a fool, but he ain't a crook. He only supervised five or six ration and allowance days whilst I was back East talking myself blue in the face to that congressional committee. Jesus, have you ever tried to explain Indian policy to a senator from New York with a drinking problem?"

"I couldn't explain it sensible to Buffalo Bill Cody. Let's get back to you getting back to find the books in order."

"I just said I did. Hutchins had issued the same rations and allowances to each and every eligible Indian. I checked to make sure they didn't try to green him, as is their wont with a new agent. But not even one squaw drew rations for the same kid twice. Hutch was smart enough to check each applicant against his official B.I.A. number."

"Did Raining Stars and his band get what was coming to them?"

"Not yet. They ain't been caught yet. But that can't be the bitch the old man had against us. Hutchins issued them the usual money and supplies just a day or so afore they run off with his wife and best horse!"

"I'll take your word the agency didn't cheat 'em. That leaves the trading post and...oh, yeah, your medical dispensary. Have they been trying to vaccinate anybody recently? Some old-fashioned Indians don't take kindly to white man's medicine, you know."

"Of course I know. I'm paid to know. And you're barking up another wrong tree, Longarm. All my wards have been vaccinated, army style, before they got here. As you know, the army don't *give* a shit about their views of preventive medicine. My medical team gets along all right with 'em. I long ago gave orders not to pester the Cheyenne. They just patch 'em up if they come asking. They usually do, once they notice how slow a rattle can cure snakebite or blood poisoning. Ain't nothing any kind of medicine man can do for consumption. So they just have to die from it, poor bastards. I've asked the B.I.A. to let me transfer consumptives out to the Arizona Territory, but it's worse than talking to a wall. Most walls at least don't tell you how little you know about consumption. They got a fancy doctor in Washington who's sure Indians get consumptive lungs from drinking hard liquor so much. I told 'em if that was true half of Texas would be dying of consumption, but—"

"Trading post," Longarm cut in. "Some greedy white traders in the past have been known to cheat Indians or, even worse, insult 'em."

Miles shook his head and said, "Not on *my* reservation.

I ain't saying white kids pay a nickel for penny candy, or that white gals buy as many ribbon bows that fade so fast in the sun. But I keep an eye on the trading post."

"While you were back East, Johnny?"

"Oh, hell, I told Hutchins to make sure nobody sold sanded sugar or sawdusted coffee while I was away. I got a trick I play on traders to keep 'em honest. I buy my own household goods and grub from the trading post, the same as my Indians. Better yet, I sometimes send an Indian over to buy it *for* me. Does that coffee taste like sawdust?"

Longarm sipped thoughtfully and said, "Nope. It's Arbuckle brand. So I reckon it's up to old Raining Stars himself to tell us what riled him. And since I hope not to be here when they bring him in, you can write me."

He stood up and added, "I'd sure like to borrow a pony and one of your Winchesters, Johnny."

Miles rose, too, saying, "Got the rifle in my office. Pick any pony and saddle you want from the police station across the way. You can leave ever'thing to be picked up at the livery nearest the depot when you get there."

Longarm said, "Thanks. Ain't going back to town directly, though. It'll take Billy Vail some time to chaw my own wire and get around to wiring back. Then I'm still stuck until the next train heading west stops in town at midnight. So as long as I'm here, I'd best sniff around some."

"Sniff away, then. What do you need with the rifle, Longarm? None of my present wards are likely to start up with you, you know."

"I know. I forgot to tell you. Some damned somebody pegged a rifle shot at Wetfeather or me on the way out. Don't know if it was an Indian or not. But I'd just as soon have a serious gun handy, should he try again."

Miles whistled softly. "I don't get it, Longarm. If you ain't serious about investigating further, how come anyone around here would be trying to stop you?"

Longarm said, "Don't know. But I sure find that an interesting question!"

Wetfeather had already driven back to town by the time Longarm and his borrowed Winchester dropped by the agency police station to borrow an Indian pony. So the two Indians on duty treated him about the way he expected they'd treat a white rider they didn't know. They tried not to grin at each other as they saddled up an innocent-looking paint stud with more quirt marks on his hide than he should have had for such a polite-looking mount. One of the Cheyenne looked just as innocent as he held the left stirrup for Longarm.

Longarm said, "No thanks. I don't think this is a good day to die," as he walked around—the front, of course—to mount from the right, Plains Indian style. The Plains Indians who had tried to slicker him into mounting an Indian-broken pony white man's style looked sort of disappointed, but just moved clear and sort of held their breath as they waited to see what would happen next.

What happened next, as Longarm had surmised it might, was that the paint went straight up in the air, twisting one way, and came down, twisting the other, to land four-legged and spine-snappy before commencing its serious scalp dance in a tight circle, throwing shoulder blocks at the stout wall of the station in passing, more than once, in case Longarm should be dumb enough to have his knee in position to bust easy.

As the show went on, stirring up clouds of dust, other Indians, male, she-male, and more childish, came from every direction to watch the fool white man get bucked off.

Longarm spoiled the fun by staying aboard as the paint, seeing he had a serious customer on his back, bucked clear of the station to give himself plenty of elbow room as he switched to sunfishing, end swapping, and, when that didn't seem to do it, trying to bite Longarm's foot off.

But Longarm's stout army boots did more damage to the paint's muzzle than the paint's snapping teeth could manage and, furthermore, once Longarm had his head down there anyway, he cranked in on the reins and held the paint's head swan-tucked so he had to buck blind if he aimed to keep bucking at all.

He did. All Cheyenne seemed to act prideful with women watching. But the trouble with bucking blind with one's swan-tucked head getting kicked silly was that it didn't work so good on a hard, wagon-rutted surface.

The brute came down awkward, busted a fetlock bone, and somersaulted ass over teakettle as Longarm dismounted gracefully as a circus rider, Winchester in hand.

He and the paint landed at about the same time, Longarm on his boot heels and the paint on his back, screaming and pawing the air wildly as all the Indians shouted in awe. Then the paint rolled over, tried to rise, and whinnied in agony as its busted bone crunched inside the skin like someone was cracking nuts. So Longarm raised the muzzle of the Winchester, levered a round in the chamber, and shot the poor critter in the head.

There was a long moment of stunned silence. Then Longarm turned to face the Indian police, smiled pleasantly, and asked, "Do you have another pony I might use, gents? This one seems a mite used up."

"You . . . You shot Old Mad Dog!" gasped the one who'd held the stirrup so politely for him.

Longarm nodded and said, "I sure did. I generally shoot anybody who's too ornery to get along with. I'd like something more like a *horse* this time, if you don't mind."

They gave him one. She was a buckskin mare who must have been watching and listening, for she acted a heap more sensibly when he climbed aboard, thanked the Indians for being so considerate, and rode on.

He didn't have far to ride. Since the junior agent, Hutchins, was making the biggest fuss about his missing wife, Longarm decided to visit him first. Hutchins was at the agency dispensary, in bed, strapped down and full of morphine. But the nurse on duty said he might be able to answer questions. So Longarm pulled up a chair near the head of the bed and said howdy.

Hutchins didn't answer. The nurse reached over Longarm to slap the doped-up agent's face hard as she said sweetly, "You have a visitor, Mr. Hutchins."

Longarm wondered where he'd heard her voice before. Her face looked sort of familiar. Her uniform, or the way she filled it, looked even more so. But it hardly seemed possible hc'd have forgotten a name to go with that sassy shape, had he ever gotten to know it in the Biblical sense.

Whoever she was, Hutchins must not have wanted her to hit him again. For he opened his eyes halfway and murmured, "Have they found Helen yet? Is she still alive?"

Longarm said, "We need your help in looking for her, Hutchins. I want you to think hard and then tell me why you think Raining Stars singled you folk out particular. Were you having trouble with the old chief just before him and his band lit out with your wife and thoroughbred?"

Hutchins rolled his eyes sort of wild and answered, "I'm not even sure which one's Raining Stars. But let me up and I'll *git* the son of a bitch!"

"Take it easy, old son. There's an army troop ahead of you in line. I know how you feel, but you got to start thinking sensibly anyway. Are you paying any attention to me at all?"

"I have to get up. I have to rescue Helen before those animals do you-know-what to her!"

Longarm didn't think it best to point out that they'd had at least a week to do anything they'd ever intended to by now. Instead he said, "Pay heed, damn it. What they done

68

was awful, but they didn't harm hair one on the heads of any other whites on this reservation. They seem to have singled you and your woman out in particular. If I could see why, I might be able to know better where to look for them and her."

"What difference does it make? Miles and the Indian police say they could have ridden off across the high plains in any direction."

"Not *any* direction. Not these days. Indians off the reserve in the company of white captives have a more limited choice than that. They could be making for the Staked Plains, the Arapaho country, or, if they're dumb as hell, they could be following Dull Knife's route north to join up with the North Cheyenne on the Rosebud Reserve. I say dumb as hell, 'cause their northern cousins will never take 'em in now. I like the Staked Plains best. But even the Comanche figure to ask 'em how come they jumped this reserve so rude. So let's study on that some more."

"God damn it, they have Helen, and while we're jawing about it like foolish geese they could be...Oh, Jesus, let me up! I got to kill me some Indians!"

Longarm turned to the nurse and asked, "Do you have to keep him so full of dope he don't make sense?"

She sighed. "You should see how he acts when he's *not* sedated! Dr. McUlric says if he doesn't come to his senses soon we'll just have to ship him east to a government asylum. Some of those newspapers back East who keep sobbing about Mister Lo, the poor Indian, should check the figures on how many whites we have locked up in nuthouses these days."

"We've driven a lot of Indians nuts, too. Meanwhile, this gent's too full of dope to question. I'd best have a word with your doc. Where's he at?"

She said, "Over at the army post. He's quarantined himself at least till the end of the month."

Longarm stared up soberly at her. "I sure hope you haven't been taking dope, too, ma'am. I wish *somebody* around here would say something sensible for a change!"

She explained, "The regular army surgeon is on leave. So cheap Uncle Sam insisted on Dr. McUlric filling in for both the army and B.I.A. until he gets back. Dr. McUlric protested, of course. But who listened?"

"Me. How come your B.I.A. doc's in quarantine? What's he caught?"

"Nothing. But in tending the sick-call roll at the army post he was exposed to measles! The soldiers will be up and about in a week or so. Do I have to tell an old Indian fighter how measles affect most Indians?"

He grimaced and said, "All the old Indian fighters put together ain't killed half as many Indians as the so-called childhood diseases our kind hardly notices. Your doc was right to protest treating whites and Indians at the same time. He's right not to come anywhere near an Indian till he knows he ain't carrying a bug that can sweep through a reserve like wildfire. But, meanwhile, what happens if some Cheyenne gets sick from some other bug, ma'am?"

"I'm in charge, of course. Don't look so superior, damn it. I made it halfway through Harvard Medical School before they ganged up on me and forced me to settle for nursing."

The penny dropped. Longarm grinned up at her and said, "Howdy, Miss Ginger. How come your hair's so black these days?"

She said, "I got tired of being called Ginger, Custis. I'd have thought you, of all people, would at least remember more than my *hair*, damn it!"

He laughed and said, "You don't have an easy figure to forget, old pard. But while I was pretty sure it was you, I was afraid of making an awesome mistake, so..."

"I knew the moment you called me 'ma'am' you'd completely forgotten me and that weekend in Denver, you brute. To save you further awkwardness, I'm still Willy May Weems, I'm still single, and I still like boys. Let's go to my quarters to finish this conversation. Mr. Hutchins, here, fades in and out sort of inconveniently."

He rose to follow Willy May, dubiously. For it was broad day, he was sort of horny from his lonely train ride from Amarillo east, and if she was the same old Willy May he'd met in Denver when she'd first come West, he wasn't going to get off with coming less than three times in her.

She led him out to the hall and down it to her own quarters, furnished mostly with a big brass bedstead. But as he took off his Stetson and started to remove his frock coat, politely, she laughed and said, "Down, boy. I'm still on duty. Can't you hold the thought until after sundown?"

She sat on the bed, patted a space beside her neighborly hips, and said, "It won't harm us to mayhaps spoon a mite. But I daren't take off my uniform till I'm sure no confounded Indian kid's likely to come in crying with a splinter in his foot. You promised me you'd write, you mean thing."

He remained standing as he assured her, "I did. But my perfumed letter come back saying you'd left without leaving a forwarding address, Willy May."

It was a flat-out lie, but she chose to believe it, saying, "Well, when I got this chance with the B.I.A. I had to jump at it. As I told you in Denver, for some reason, men just don't seem to want me in the medical profession."

He didn't answer. It wouldn't have been polite to say he suspected they hadn't wanted her in that hospital in Denver because a well-proportioned nurse who screwed so willing would likely complicate life for the rest of the medical staff. He wondered who she was messing with here. But that wouldn't have been polite to mention, either.

She asked, "Don't you even want to kiss me, damn it?"

He said, *"Want* to. Ain't sure we'd better start just yet.

71

As you may recall, Willy May, we're both sort of weak-natured, once we get started."

She laughed lewdly. "I'll get you for that come sundown. How long will you be here, Custis?"

"Don't know. On the one hand, this case has turned into the sort of mess the Justice Department usually leaves to the War Department. On the other hand, some son of a bitch tried to bushwhack me on the way out here today, and that can't be constitutional. Let's talk about the Indians running off with that white gal, for openers. What can you tell me about Helen Hutchins, Willy May?"

The voluptuous nurse shrugged. "I didn't get to know her all that well before it happened. She was a pretty little thing, if you like your women mostly skin and bones."

He grinned down at her and said, "You know what kind of woman I like. But hold on. Did you say she was *little?* An Indian just described her to me as *tall* and *skinny.*"

Willy May said, "They don't wear high heels. So all white women seem a mite taller to an Indian than they really are. I guess Helen Hutchins would stand about five six, naked. I guess they have her naked right about now, right?"

He grimaced and replied, "If she's still alive and if that's why they carried her off. No offense, Willy May, you're a hell of a well-stacked she-male and most Indians like their squaws a mite plump. But *you're* still here, safe and sound. So tell me true, remembering we're old pals and that I don't shock easy, have any of the young bucks been blowing nose flutes under your windows at night of late?"

"Good God, I know I practically raped you that time in Denver, but a girl has to have *some* standards! Besides, they treat all us whites as strangers. Most are polite enough. Some, to be fair, are even friendly. But I fear I've been true to you alone since coming down here."

She sort of wriggled her sitting parts on the edge of the

72

mattress and closed her eyes sensuously as she added, "What time is it, Custis?"

"Early afternoon. Hold the thought. You say you didn't know the Hutchins woman well, so there's no sense speculating on whether or not some buck was hankering for her particular. But if he was, he sure had it narrowed down some. Are there any other good-looking white gals out here at this agency, Willy May?"

She shrugged and said grudgingly, "The trader's wife isn't bad-looking. But I know for a fact she hasn't been screwing around with Indians. Or anyone else, poor thing. She comes to me regular for a prescription."

"You mean she's got problems with her plumbing?"

"No. Far from it. Her husband has. She married a man old enough to be her father and, as any medically trained person can tell you, that's not always a good idea for a naturally warm-natured young woman." Then she frowned thoughtfully and added, "Oh, Christ, why did I tell you that, you randy bastard?"

He chuckled. "Because I'm investigating a mystery, and I thank you, even though you're making it even more mysterious. Indians have more contact with the reservation nurse, traders, schoolteachers, and such than they might with the agent's housewife. Oh, I forgot. What does your *schoolmarm* look like?"

"Old, ugly, and male." She laughed, adding, "He's not here now, anyway. Summer vacation."

He laughed back. "Two out of three ain't bad, and it's still a mystery why they took a gal they hardly knew and didn't even consider you or the good-looking trader gal. Wait, I take that back. They might have considered you two, but had a better reason for paying back Hutchins for some real or imagined slight. Miles says the books don't show nothing to indicate Hutchins was mistreating the In-

73

dians. But the Indians recall his wife as stuck-up. Tell me if I'm getting warm."

"*I'm* getting warm as hell for this early in the day, damn it." She sighed. "Helen Hutchins was stuck-up, but not in a nasty way. She just kept to herself. Hardly ever left her house and didn't invite anyone in much. They had the same Osage housekeeper as the head agent. She's still here. It couldn't have been a servant problem, and Indians don't expect to be invited to tea, so . . ."

"Let's get to the Indians who ran off. What can you tell me about Raining Stars and his band over to Cottontail Draw? Any of 'em ever come to you folks here, sick?"

Willy May grimaced and said, "Most of them were sick all the time. But you know how some Indians are. Dr. McUlric and I drove out to the draw last winter after hearing they had fever in their camp. They might have. Old Raining Stars chased us away before we could examine anyone. He seems to think he's a medicine man as well as a kidnapper and a horse thief. He said there was nothing white man's medicine could do for his defeated nation. Whoever said blue eyes are colder than brown never looked a very bitter old Indian in the face, Custis. Dr. McUlric said he was either running a temperature or about to explode from pure combustion. But, as he wouldn't even let us check his pulse, we got out of there before anyone could get really ugly."

"You say you and the doc riled the old gent. Yet neither of you was pestered as you rode off. Could the gal as was have ridden out there and mayhaps pestered them *worse?*"

Willy May thought. "She did ride about a lot on that thoroughbred they couldn't really afford. But I was under the impression she rode mostly into town or over to the army post, when they were having social functions at the officer's club. She was a sort of . . . well . . . fancy Eastern gal. Frankly, I don't think she liked the country out here, let alone the Indians. I just can't see her making social calls to Cottontail Draw. It's a good ride to nowhere much. Living in a tipi may not be so bad when one moves at least once a month. But have you ever smelled an Indian camp with no sanitary facilities after it's stayed put a spell?"

Longarm grimaced and replied, "A tipi ring does get gamy, even moving some. I can't see a prissy white gal who didn't speak a word of Cheyenne going out of her way to visit sullen, unsanitary ones. Not when you say she didn't even socialize with the more assimilated Cheyenne here at the agency. But, sullen as he might have been, Raining Stars must have at least thought he had a reason for carrying off both that fine horse and its rider. Had they just wanted the horse, they'd have found the gal by now, in one condition or another. And, come to think of it, why would a Plains Indian want a sissy thoroughbred, broken white?"

"Well, it was a mighty pretty horse, Custis."

"Cheyenne don't judge horseflesh by pretty. Not riding on the warpath. Have you ever had the feeling that an important piece of the puzzle is from another jigsaw entirely? Everybody tells me the same basic facts, but I just can't make 'em fit no matter how I twist and turn 'em."

Willy May was twisting and turning her bottom on the bed as she said in a husky voice, "I don't think anyone's likely to need medical attention for at least fifteen minutes, dear, do you?"

He wasn't sure fifteen minutes would do her. But as she seemed to be unbuttoning the front of her uniform at the moment, she must have thought so. He sighed and said, "Well, it's sort of hot out, right now, for serious investigating."

Then he heard a tinny bugle blowing in the distance, but not fifteen minutes away, and said, "Damn, here comes the army!"

"Custis," she pleaded, "I'm gushing for your old-fashioned loving, and for all we know they'll ride on by!"

He shook his head wistfully and said, "I've likely had more bugles blowed at me than you, honey. so you'd best take my word they just swung toward this agency. I'd best go over to join Johnny Miles and see what's up."

"I was hoping you'd be up and in me by now, you mean thing!"

"I was, too. But hope springs eternal and you have my word we'll do it right later tonight. So please don't start without me, Willy May. If I ain't back by sundown my fool pecker will never forgive me, neither!"

For some fool reason she threw a glass from her bed table at the door as he closed it after him and legged out to mount up and trot the mare the short distance to the head-quarters building. He got there first, to find John Miles and Whitepony waiting at the foot of the porch steps. Whitepony asked, "Why did you shoot that paint pony, Longarm? The boys are mad as hell at you about that."

Longarm dismounted and tethered the buckskin to the porch rail as he replied, "That's fair. I'm mad at them, too. When you skin Old Mad Dog out you'll find he busted his own off leg trying to bust my ass. I shot him 'cause somebody had to. No offense, but it was about time. Do you always treat guests so ornery out here, Whitepony?"

The Indian smiled sheepishly and said, "Aw, they were just having a little fun with you. I'll tell 'em you shot the pony for a reason instead of just to get even. Wetfeather told me when he picked me up in town that somebody took a shot at you as well today."

"They may have been aiming at him. I assume we're all standing here in the hot sun because of that same bugle call?"

Miles said, "Yeah. The army likes to let folks know they're coming long before they're in sight. Likely makes Indian fighting more interesting on the rolling prairie."

Whitepony pointed with his chin. "I see their dust now

and . . . yes, there they come, over that rise, lined up like ducks in a shooting gallery. How on earth did you ever lick us, Longarm?"

"Just lucky, I reckon. Who's them two Indians with 'em? The Pawnee you mentioned before?"

"Yes. Look at them, riding like squaws. I'll bet they didn't even find a fresh cow turd."

Whitepony was correct in his assumption, it turned out, when the cavalry patrol and their Pawnee scouts reined in. Although, to Longarm, the Pawnee didn't look all that sissy. They looked more as if someone had stuck the heads of wooden Indians atop trail-dusted cowhands. For though, like most Indian scouts, they were dressed shabby white, the Pawnee had stuck to the shaved heads and scalp roaches most whites associated with the Mohawk farther east. Pawnee and Cheyenne didn't speak the same Indian lingo. So Whitepony taunted them in English, asking, "How did your rabbit hunt go, my Pawnee brothers?"

One of the Pawnee smiled pleasantly and said, "I don't see how I could have a Cheyenne brother. My mother and father were married."

The young white lieutenant in command of the patrol told them to knock it off as he told his troopers to dismount and smoke if they had 'em. Then he dismounted himself and limped over to tell Miles, "Not a trace of the red rascals, sir. We circled the site of that massacre. My Indians had no trouble reading the trail those poor dead drovers left coming north out of Texas. But the band that hit them must have been riding big-ass birds. Not a hoof mark anywhere that hadn't obviously been left by the victims and their herd."

Longarm took out a cheroot and lit it before he observed laconically, "The trail herders were riding shod ponies. They came north during or just after that wet spell we had about a week ago. They likely gathered the herd near water and

77

green brush, waiting to see if the storm was over, or if they were just in the eye of it. It was just a summer squall, if it hit down here like it hit up Denver way. So let's say a band riding unshod lighter ponies came along just as the ground was drying hard again. That might work."

The young officer shot him a curious look. Miles introduced them, adding that Longarm had scouted Indians in his time. One of the Pawnee had been listening, scowling, and cut in impolitely, "Hear me, mighty white tracker: you were not there. *We* were. You are full of shit. Those white drovers were hit *before* that storm you are so sure about, not after. What have you to say now, great keen-eyed reader of sign you've never seen!"

Longarm smiled back thinly and replied, "I am waiting for some mighty Pawnee warrior to tell me how he knows so much about things that happened over a week ago when *none* of us were there."

The Pawnee said, "We know the rain came after the attack because silt was washed into hoof- and boot-prints by the rain. The bodies and recovered stock were taken to the army post days ago, of course. But you can still see where the white men lay dead in the grass. The grass they covered with their bodies is clean. The grass all around is gray with silt washed over it by the hard rain. Even you would have been able to read *that* much, since I see you don't wear glasses. Hear me: we found no hoofprints leading away from the scene of the slaughter. But, since we didn't find the runaway band there waiting for us, they must have gone somewhere. Why don't you tell us how they got their ponies to fly, big white scout?"

Before Longarm could try, the Cheyenne policeman, Whitepony, laughed scornfully and said, "Easy. You say you read hoofmarks leading into the camp of the dead whites. I think I was barely old enough to talk when my grandfather told me how Crooked Lances used to walk their ponies

78

backwards along a trail, and Raining Stars is a Crooked Lance! Am I speaking too fast for you, Pawnee offspring of at least first cousins?"

The Pawnee cursed in his own lingo and snapped in English, "Watch your mouth, Cheyenne sister-fucker!"

So the other, less excited Pawnee cut in to explain more politely, "We thought of that. The scattered herd had milled over the sign leading north. It was possible a small band could have used that old trick. But not thirty or more. And Raining Stars left here with that many ponies and, of course, the big steel-shod horse of their white captive."

Longarm asked, "Is there any law saying Raining Stars couldn't have left most of his band in another draw and just hit them cowhands with a modest force, say on foot?"

The Pawnee scouts looked at one another, sort of chagrined.

The white officer said, "That works, up to a point. But we didn't start scouting from the massacre site like sniffing hounds. We circled wide, then wider. We scouted all the nearby draws, then we scouted farther out. We didn't find a thing, not even a patch of charred sod where they might have made camp, for half a day's ride in every direction!"

The more sensible Pawnee said, "Hear me: I told you before, Blue Sleeves. We should not waste time scouting for sign. It is easy to tell where they are going. We should be riding north, toward the Rosebud, not back to the post empty-handed!"

The lieutenant said, "And I told *you*, my orders were to get a line on which way they might be headed and report back, not chase wild geese all the way to the darned Dakotas! Face facts, Long Walker. They could just as easily be headed due west or even south."

The Pawnee shook his head. "Hear me: they have brothers up at the Rosebud. There is noplace else for them to go."

The young officer turned to Miles and Longarm. "He may be right, but I have orders. We'd best get back to the post and put it on the wire. Army units to the north are in better position than us to head 'em off, if that's where they're headed."

Longarm just nodded. There was an outside chance Raining Stars would act that foolish. Willy May had said he'd been acting wild-eyed earlier. But, as the patrol mounted up and rode on, he turned to Miles and Whitepony to say, "You'd best alert the Comache and Arapaho agencies, Johnny. In the Shining Times, as you doubtless recall, the South Cheyenne rode more with Arapaho and Comanche than their northern cousins. The North Cheyenne were part of the Lakota Confederacy. The South Cheyenne weren't."

Miles nodded grimly and said, "I'm betting on the Co-manche and the Staked Plains, seeing what that southbound milled-over trail might mean. Jesus, if Raining Stars gets to Quanna Parker and convinces him he's had a strong medicine vision..."

Longarm shrugged. "Last I heard, old Quanna's living white and in the real-estate business. But there's more than one old unreconstructed Comanche left, and Raining Stars must have said *something* important to get them other Chey-enne to leave such a nice, well-run agency. By the way, as long as I'm here, could I copy down the names and B.I.A. numbers of the other runaways? Nurse Willy May says the old man didn't look too healthy, last time anyone looked. So we'd best consider who's likely to fill his moccasins, should he come down with the measles or something."

Miles nodded and led Longarm inside. He didn't invite Whitepony in, so Whitepony didn't follow. Inside, Longarm asked if Miles was sore at him. Miles shrugged and said, "He's all right, I reckon. But, face it, he ain't rooting for our side."

"Oh? He mentioned something about us not trusting Cheyenne to track Cheyenne. Seemed a mite angry about it, too."

"Can't say I blame him, but I don't make the rules. Come on, I got the files in my office. Want Funny Eyes to coffee you some more?"

"No, thanks. She just did. But that reminds me—wouldn't a Cheyenne trying to recapture lost glory consider riding off with an Osage gal a sort of coup? In the Shining Times, the more dangerous a captured woman's nation was, the greater the glory, and the Osage are still mean as hell to folks who steal their squaws and ponies."

Miles sat at his rolltop desk and rummaged through its drawers as he muttered, "Jesus, Longarm, there you go trying to think like a damned Indian again. How the hell are *we* supposed to know what goes on in a wild Indian's head?"

Longarm pulled up a chair for himself and sat down. "Sometimes it helps at least to try, Johnny. When I'm hunting rabbit I don't have to turn myself into a rabbit to know the critter's sure to circle back if I just hunker down and wait a spell. I don't even have to know *why* it thinks it should. I just have to know it *does*."

Miles got out a ledger and spread it on his desk. "I follow you. I agree that these particular Cheyenne don't seem to be thinking or acting Cheyenne. But they ain't. So let's let *them* figure it out. Here's the family heads as was camped with Raining Stars out to Cottontail Draw, speaking of rabbits. As you can see, fourteen lodges full of thirty-three men and women drawed the rations and allowances as was coming to them."

Longarm took out his own notebook and a pencil stub, rested the ledger across his knees, and started transcribing. "Who would have come in to pick up, Johnny?" he asked.

"Each family head, of course. As you can see, there's an X, an arrowhead, or whatever next to each name and B.I.A. number. Fourteen in all. Ain't no Indian at *this* agency picking up bread, beans, and cold cash without showing his I.D. and signing for it."

"Yeah, but each family head draws according to the number of dependents he has."

"All right, so there's always a *little* graft. But look again and you'll see that particular band only drawed for nineteen extra mouths to feed and clothe."

"Just did. Most folk have more kids underfoot than that. How come old Raining Stars and his pals had so few kids, Johnny?"

"They didn't have any *little* kids at all. The five left over after wives is extra wives or growed sons and daughters still living at home. Raining Stars wasn't the only old Crooked Lancer out to Cottontail Draw. It was almost an Indian home for the aged. Save for the few teenagers, they was all hold-outs from the Shining Times. Hardly any of 'em less'n forty. Some older. Younger Cheyenne would rather live in sensible houses now. Have you ever spent a winter night in a damned old tipi, Longarm?"

"Yeah, with two squaws, and I still come close to freezing my balls. They sure must have hated living out the rest of their days our way."

"Hell, if they'd been anxious to get civilized, they wouldn't have acted so ornery. I wonder which of 'em's screwing that white gal about now."

"Dirty old men can get silly, too, Johnny. Can't see Raining Stars himself as a mad rapist. The spirit may be willing, but the poor old bastard must be over sixty. And that's old for a primitive-living white man. I don't think that's why they stole her. Says here they all drew on the B.I.A. for squaws as well. One squaw at least for every man in the band. And while some old men are dirty old men, old women are generally jealous as hell."

"What about a teenage buck?"

"Growed to manhood on a reserve, without a coup feather to call his own, telling his elders, and them Crooked Lancers, what he even meant to eat for breakfast?"

Miles nodded. "All right. They run into her riding her fool horse as they was running off, sneaky. They took her along a ways, then killed her. It's agreed they must have been in a surly mood at the time."

Longarm shook his head and said, "Let's credit even Pawnee trackers with more skill than that, Johnny. If she lay buried within a day's ride of the reservation line, *someone* would have found her by now."

"Mebbe. What if she was killed and buried *on* the reserve? It's big as hell, and, as you say, they started searching for sign along the *edges!*"

Longarm sighed. "I wish you wouldn't say things like that, old son. Aside from being sort of grim to study on, it *works.*"

Chapter 6

Finding his way to Cottontail Draw was easy enough for Longarm. It was after he got there, tethered his Indian pony, and started scouting for sign that it got tedious.

It wasn't as if there was no sign to scout. There was *too* much. The now-missing tipi ring still smelled awful. Each missing tipi's position was clearly visible as a big flat cow chip of dead ashes, beef bones, empty tin cans, and worse. The camp had been on a sandy flood terrace of the draw, with the main channel, now dry, at a tolerably safe lower level. The slopes to either side were brushy with cut and resprouted willow. Like most born nomads, the Indians had used anywhere they felt like in the surrounding brush as a place to squat and drop it. This worked out a lot better when one moved camp every once in a while. Most of the leavings were little more than patches of killed, discolored grass, now. But a sickly, acrid odor hung in the still air all around. He found nothing of value or even interest left in the draw by the vanished Indians. So he scouted wider, found nothing but summer-dried grass on the ridges to either side, and hunkered down on a rise to smoke and study, staring morosely down at the deserted camp below. It was easier to see why they'd left it than it was to see why they'd ever wanted to live there at all. Despite its name, he'd spotted no sign of cottontail in or about Cottontail Draw, and old buffalo hunters couldn't have been too excited about eating rabbit in any case. Not when the Great White Father issued them beef, even scrawny beef.

He shook his head and told himself, *They wasn't driven out by hunger. They'd just been issued rations and cash to buy more with. They didn't seem interested in the beef them drovers was keeping company with when they jumped 'em. Meanwhile, old son, where would you bury a white gal, and maybe her horse, around here?*

He got up and moved on to look, but he didn't find anything. The prairie sod around the draw was thick and unbroken. The recent unseasonable rain had greened the grass stems at their bases some, and grass grew faster over dug-up, watered, and, in this case, fertilized ground. The same rain would have left a shallow dimple in the sand below had it been disturbed the other side of the storm. While if anyone had broken the surface *this* side of the storm the sand grains wouldn't have been so uniformly covered by a thin wash of silt. Had anything bigger than a dog been buried under the willows, they'd be wilting about it now. But all the fresh willow buds were the same size, so their roots were all stuck in the same kind of dirt.

He gave up and headed back to where he'd left the buckskin. A redskin was waiting for him there. He said, "Howdy, Miss Funny Eyes. What brings you here?"

"The agent has ridden into town," the Osage girl said. "He left a message for you. I was afraid you might not come back to the agency, so I brought it out to you. They said at the trading post you had asked the way out here to Cottontail Draw."

"I did, and it seems a smart walk for a gal on foot, Miss Funny Eyes. But at least I can ride you back, pillion. What's the message?"

She handed him a folded scrap of paper. "I don't know. I can't read. But I thought it might be important," she told him.

He thanked her and unfolded the note to read: "Went to town to wire my fool woman. May stay a while. Help yourself to anything you want till I get back. If that includes Funny Eyes, don't tell me about it later. I ain't supposed to allow that, you rascal. Miles."

He chuckled and put the note away. The pretty little Osage asked, "Was it important?"

"Sort of," he said. "You're sure you don't read at all?"

"Only a few words. Not long ones, like you people. What does riding pillion mean?"

"The gal sits in back, on the saddle skirts. But let's not be in a hurry. I've been anxious to jaw with an Indian who don't owe the Cheyenne Crooked Lance Society even sentimental feelings. Let's mosey up the draw, away from this garbage dump."

He untethered the buckskin and led it on foot as Funny Eyes fell in beside him, saying, "Don't Cheyenne smell terrible? My people are cleaner. Over in the Osage Strip, we've been living like white people for a long time."

He said, "I noticed, last time I was over that way. The agent says you run away from home, though. How come, Funny Eyes?"

She sighed. "My family wished for me to marry an old man. He had many cattle, many. But it was silly. I remembered sitting on his lap when I was a little girl. It would have been like marrying my own grandfather. I like younger, prettier men. I could never marry a man too old and feeble to . . . to treat a woman right."

"Well, mayhaps when you're a mite older you'll see the advantages of wealth better. Most gals seem to, bless their practical little hides. But let's talk about the folk at the trading post."

"I feel sorry for that poor white girl, married to a man so old," she said.

"They seemed happy enough with each other," Longarm

86

said. "That ain't what I wanted to ask about. When I dropped by for directions, they told me they hadn't sold much in the way of anything to the band as was camped back there since last fall. Does that make sense to you?"

She shrugged and said, "I did not know the people camped out here. They seldom came in and, when they did, they looked daggers at everyone, even Indians. They say the old man who led them had visions, many visions. He just looked like a ragged old Cheyenne to me. My people wear nice clothes. Mostly your kind. Even when the old ones dress up the old way for ceremonies, they wear nice fringed buckskins and clean feathers. I think these Cheyenne have sick hearts. They act like beaten people."

"Well, maybe that's the way they feel. You Osage got licked long enough ago to have forgotten your own Shining Times. Licked or not, anyone has to eat. But the trader says they ain't bought so much as a can of beans for months. It gets even spookier, considering, when he swears he ain't sold them a round of hunting ammo since last fall."

"You don't need bullets to hunt rabbit and groundhog," Funny Eyes said. "There aren't many deer left to hunt around here. Maybe they just had no money to buy things at the trading post."

He shook his head. "That's even spookier. They had lots of money when they jumped the reserve. They weren't too proud to come in for their allowance all winter and spring. But they didn't even buy a round of .22 Short with it. Yet here they are on the warpath?"

They rounded a bend and Funny Eyes said, "That patch of grass looks inviting, don't you think?"

"Yeah, it surely does. But I'm still thinking about the spooky way old Raining Stars and his people were acting, just before they lit out."

She moved ahead to sit in the thick dry grass, not paying as much attention to her skirts as she might have as she locked her elbows around her knees, smiled languidly up at him. "Maybe they were saving their money to *buy* ammunition," she suggested.

He let go the reins to let the buckskin graze at will as he sat down beside her. "Thanks. That makes sense. I figured an Indian might think more sneaky than me. Had Raining Stars started buying out all the ammunition at the trading post, the trader would have naturally mentioned it to Johnny Miles or Hutchins. But that would have brought about the same results with an army post just a short ride away. Yeah, that might explain the sudden thrift. I reckon even I could live on rabbit a spell if I set out enough snares in the willows all around. It could explain why they wouldn't let the nurse and Doc McUlric inside any tipis, even if some of 'em were feeling poorly last winter."

She took his free hand and placed it in her lap, saying, "I am tired of talking about old, unwashed Cheyenne. Did you know that among my people, in the old days, the maiden got to choose her own lovers?"

He said he'd figured as much, although he was too polite to add he doubted like hell she was a maiden as they fell back together in the grass by mutual unspoken consent.

She kissed the same as any white gal would have, if she'd known how to kiss French. But when Longarm put an exploring hand up under her skirts, and found she was built just the same as any white gal not wearing underdrawers, Funny Eyes said, "Wait, I don't want to rumple my maid's costume. Let me take it off."

That sounded fair, though he felt a little awkward undressing in broad daylight. He didn't mind *her* admiring him in his birthday suit, but he sure figured to feel silly should anyone ride over the rise to either side. So he made sure his gun rig lay neatly folded, .44 grips up, in the grass by her left ear, before he rolled aboard Funny Eyes to see if she did *everything* so white.

She gasped in surprised delight as he entered her and proceeded to move her hips in a manner any gal of any race would be hard put to match. As he returned the compliment she moaned, "Harder, harder, pound me into the ground, sweet white lover!"

"Are you sure I ain't hurting your sassy little tailbone, you sassy little thing?"

"It hurts good! Hear me: I haven't had a man since I left the Osage Strip, and I was hard up when I left!"

He felt sure she was telling the truth as she climaxed way ahead of him and kept beating the ground like a tom-tom with her rollicking rump, gasping, "Kiss me! Kiss me with your tongue! You are driving me crazy with desire! Make love to me, you fool!"

He'd thought, up to now, that was what he was doing. But if she wanted to play rough, he was willing. So he proceeded to pound hell out of her.

They came together this time. She wrapped her tawny legs and naked arms around him and swore she'd kill him if he ever stopped. So, not wanting to die, he kept screwing her until she gasped, "Oh, yes! I'm about to come again!"

But just as Longarm raised his weight on locked elbows to do her right, with her smiling lovingly up at him, a bullet hit her right where her long black hair was parted!

Longarm rolled off, grabbing his gun, as the second rifle bullet tore through the dead girl's left breast. Then Longarm was firing back at the blue haze of rifle smoke against the sky upslope as he called it every lowdown thing he could think of. The killer didn't answer, not even with another rifle shot. So Longarm leaped to his bare feet and charged up the rise, reloading from the rig he carried in his free hand as he did so. He got to the top just in time to see a distant rider on a bay going over the crest of the next rise to the west. He yelled, "Come back and fight like a skunk, at least, you yellow-livered squaw-killer!"

But the distant rider didn't look back, even as Longarm emptied another cylinder after him at what he knew was impossible range.

Then Longarm was standing naked and alone under an accusing, empty sky. He sobbed with rage, cursed the whole cruel, uncaring world, and headed down to where he'd left the pretty little squaw.

He dressed quickly. Then, since it was all he could do for a pal now, he got her own duds back on her body. He took out his jackknife and ripped her bodice open, so as to account for her breast taking the round more modestly. Then he picked her up tenderly and said, "I'm sure sorry as hell about this, honey. But with luck we can still save your reputation some. Nobody but your murderer knows what you were doing when he killed you. And when I catch up with that son of a bitch, *he* won't be talking much about any lady, ever!"

Longarm brought the body in to the agency face down across the saddle. He gave the Indian police the note she'd carried out to him and anyone could see she hadn't been gone long enough to do much more than get shot by a person or persons unknown. Whitepony did say, "I don't understand why they shot her instead of you, unless the two of you were standing mighty close." But he seemed satisfied when Longarm said, "Hell, they shot her *twice,* and she was carrying a message to me."

Whitepony looked at the scrap of paper again. "Yes, and part of it seems to be torn off. I recognize John Miles's handwriting. He says you are to help yourself to anything at his house until he gets back. But there the message is ripped off. What else could he have written?"

"We'll ask him when he gets back. It might have been something the killer didn't want us to read. It might have been less important than the killer thought. Hell, it could

90

have just got tore off by a bullet. I didn't look for missing parts. Just found what's there balled up in the poor little gal's hand. Let's get down to more important missing details. Miles rode to town. Hutchins is strapped in bed. You and these other gents have been right here for a spell, I hope?"

Whitepony nodded. "We just ate together, sitting in this dooryard in the shade, and in considerable view all around, when you get around to asking. The trader and his woman haven't left their store all day and the only riding horse they own between them is a dapple gray, not a bay."

"That still leaves a whole Indian tribe unaccounted for, and I'm sure some damned body on this reserve must own at least one bay horse, damn it!"

Whitepony nodded. "You'll find at least three out back in the corral. Go feel their muzzles if you won't take an Indian's word."

"I never said I doubted you, Whitepony. So let's stop mean-mouthing each other and concentrate on the mean bastard who shot this poor little Osage gal! By the way, what are the rules on burying Osage proper?"

A sullen-looking Cheyenne in the modest but rapidly growing crowd around them muttered, "Ship her back to the Osage Strip and let *them* worry about it. Osage are just some sort of Sioux, anyway."

But a fat old woman in the crowd called him something awful in Cheyenne and came forward, saying, "Hear me: my mother was Lakota, or, as this idiot calls them, Sioux. The Osage do follow the same customs, and I know them. Give the poor child to my sisters and me. We will see that she is sent to the Old Woman's Lodge under the Northern Lights in the manner of her people!"

Longarm nodded, too busy swallowing the lump in his throat to answer. So the old lady started yelling orders in Cheyenne and in no time at all poor little Funny Eyes was being carried off tenderly by a mess of squaws bawling like she was their dead daughter or, more likely, an honored guest of the Cheyenne Nation.

Whitepony rubbed a knuckle against his eyes, likely trying to get out a speck of dust, and said, "We'd better find you a new saddle. That one has blood on it."

Longarm shook his head. "It's dry now, and I'm wearing brown pants anyway. I ain't got time to stand on ceremony. Got to get into town and wire my office."

"To tell them about the killing of Funny Eyes?"

"No. To tell 'em I won't be headed back to Denver now after all."

He started to remount. Then he stopped, frowned thoughtfully, and asked Whitepony, "How come I got to ride to town? Johnny Miles had to ride in, too, to wire his wife back East."

Whitepony shrugged. "Ain't that where the Western Union is?"

Longarm said, "It is. But most Indian agencies I've visited have their *own* telegraph set. How come you don't have one here?"

"Don't look at me. I just work for the B.I.A., I don't run it. Ask Miles, when you see him in town."

Longarm nodded, mounted the buckskin, and said, "I mean to. By the way, what kind of a horse did he ride into town just now? Do you know?"

Whitepony sighed. "I was hoping you wouldn't ask that. Miles always rides the same bay gelding. But you don't think he'd shoot at another white man, do you, Longarm?"

Longarm didn't answer as he rode off. The son of a bitch he was after hadn't just shot a white man. He'd murdered an Indian gal, and a pretty one to boot! Longarm wasn't going to let him off for poor marksmanship. Murder was murder. Killing anyone called for a hanging. That was the law.

But as Longarm followed the wagon trace toward town, he saw that, this time at least, he might have to bend the law a mite.

The trouble with hanging a son of a bitch was that he got to tell his own side in open court first. So, while Longarm doubted any jury was likely to consider shooting naked ladies a proper or even sensible defense, for the sake of poor little Funny Eyes, and her relations back in the Osage Strip, he'd just have to gun her killer on sight, and to hell with what he had to say for himself.

He knew Billy Vail wouldn't approve. But what Billy Vail didn't know wouldn't hurt him. And it wasn't as if the killer deserved to be treated *human*, now!

He lit a smoke and told his mount, "You may have to witness for me, Buck. For, if the bastard spoils things by offering to come quiet, it'll be just between me and you horses, once I get him alone on the trail. Ain't it a bitch how often prisoners try to escape from a poor old boy just trying to do his job?"

Chapter 7

The stable boy at the livery near the depot confirmed that John D. Miles had indeed ridden into town on a bay gelding. After that it was all downhill. The horse inside was cool and content. Miles had checked his saddle carbine with the kid for safekeeping and, when Longarm flashed his badge and the stable boy brought him the gun, a quick sniff and a peek down the bore told Longarm the carbine hadn't been cleaned, let alone fired, in recent memory. Besides which, it was chambered for the usual .44-40 Remington rounds, and poor little Funny Eyes had been hit with something more serious, like a .50 Express. But, as long as he had a cooperative witness, Longarm asked the stable hand what time Miles had left his bay there and, more important, if he'd checked it out for a short errand since.

The boy shook his head. "He asked me to rub it down and oat it. Hasn't been back to see if I done it yet. I can't swear to the time, since we charge by the day. But if it's any help, Mr. Miles rode in two, three hours ago."

Longarm nodded and said, "It helps. You start by scratching names off your list so's you can look closer at them that's left. Has anybody rid a horse of the same color in more recent?"

"You mean a bay? Hell, three outten four cow ponies is bay, Deputy."

"I know, damn it. Let's try her this way. Has anyone

you may or may not know rid in within the last hour or so on a lathered, hard-rid bay?"

The stable boy shook his head and said, "I'd have told you if anyone had. I ain't stupid. Anyone can see you're looking for someone less than an hour ahead of you on a bay gelding."

Longarm smiled thinly. "Didn't get close enough to examine the horse's balls. But I am mighty interested in the comings and goings of a white man or an Indian dressed white, aboard a big bay whatever, armed with a high-powered rifle. Likely a double-barreled Express rifle, since I'm still alive."

He reached in his pocket and got out four bits. "I know a dime is the usual, but there's more where this comes from if you keep your eyes peeled for a rider like I just described. If he comes here, don't say nothing stupid to him. Don't run looking for me. Just stable his mount and go on about your business till I get back to you, hear?"

The stable boy grinned and put the four bits in his jeans. "I got one more question," Longarm said. "No offense, but are you an Indian or a Mex?"

The boy frowned defensively. "I'm an American, damn it! My pa was Kiowa and my ma was as white as you. Soon as I was old enough to ride, my ma and me escaped. What's it to you?"

"Nothing, long as I know you ain't in the files of the B.I.A. or, worse yet, a Cheyenne spy. I think you're American as me, too, pard. So keep a sharp eye on your other customers and we'll talk some more when I come back for the buckskin."

Having eliminated the Indian agent for now, Longarm crossed to the Western Union office to see if his home office had anything to say to him.

Billy Vail had wired him to come on back, agreeing that the habits of Raining Stars had gotten too disgusting for anyone but the army to worry about.

Longarm grabbed a telegram blank and wrote back about how interesting the situation had become since last they'd discussed it. He asked permission to stay a spell and investigate the murder of a government ward on federal property. Then, to make sure he had some time, no matter what the home office decided, he told the clerk to send it night-letter rates.

The clerk said, "They won't get it before Monday if you send this as a night letter, Deputy. Tomorrow's the Sabbath and the Denver office won't deliver till Monday morn at the earliest."

"That's all right," Longarm said. "Nobody will be in the office of a Sunday, anyways. Tell me something. Since you're so interested in what folk might or might not be wiring home, did John D. Miles from the Cheyenne agency just wire home to his family back East?"

"I'm not supposed to discuss private messages with strangers, Deputy."

"Oh, hell, I ain't a stranger. I'm a federal officer investigating crimes too numerous to mention. So let's try that again and see if you can't be more patriotic."

The clerk sighed and said, "You're supposed to get a court order. But, since you likely can, I may as well tell you I just sent a wire to Mrs. John D. Miles and that, yes, her husband sent it."

"What did he have to say to her?"

"Now that, damn it, is pushing your luck. I could lose my job letting you read other people's love letters!"

"You could lose your job if the federal government told Western Union to fire you, too. They got lots of wires across public domain to consider. But you don't have to tell me every mushy word. Just tell me Johnny Miles wired innocent to his old lady and nobody else, and we'll say no more about it."

96

The clerk shrugged. "All right. I guess I can give you the gist, since I saw nothing sinister in either of the wires he sent."

"Either of 'em? He sent two?"

"Sure. He wired a mushy message to his wife, allowing he missed her some and that she'd best get out here pronto if she didn't want him turning squaw man. Then he sent a message to the B.I.A. about them missing Indians of his. He said the army can't seem to find 'em. And, oh, yeah, he said he suspects someone's trying to impede the investigation by sniping at folks on or about the reserve. Unless he's just got a loco Indian hater or a crazy Indian on his hands as well. He mentioned you, too, favorable, but said he feared you'd be leaving, since chasing open-and-shut renegade Indians ain't your job. I can't think of anything else he said to anyone that would be of any help to you, Deputy."

Longarm said, "Neither can I. But tell me something. How come the B.I.A. uses Western Union instead of their own telegraph here at Fort Reno? Most agencies have their own, you know."

The Western Union man nodded. "Most agencies have to, since they're mostly so far from our regular offices. When Dull Knife and his band jumped the Fort Reno reserve a year or so ago they cut all the wires they come to, riding north. I reckon Washington feels it costs the taxpayers less if we repair our own lines with our own private funds. So they never got around to replacing the agency lines. As you see, it's easy enough for the agent to wire home here by the depot, or over to the army post."

"They have a line east from the army garrison?"

"Sort of. It splices into our lines when it reaches 'em. Why?"

"Just jawing. Half the questions a lawman has to ask don't lead nowhere important. But we gotta ask 'em anyway. One more thing: has Western Union itself had any wires mysteriously out since Raining Stars got lost, strayed, or stolen?"

The Western Union man shook his head. "That storm we had about a week or so ago played hell with the wires across the High Plains. But we got 'em all up again now. Why?"

"Just filling in more blanks. Your average wire crew consists of no more'n five or six men, right?"

"Sure. Sometimes less, if the break's close to town. Tracing a break out on open range, they naturally take along a combined chuck and supply wagon. Couple of shotgun messengers, too, in case they meet up with unpleasant gents out in the middle of nowheres. But that don't happen often."

Longarm nodded soberly and said, "In this case it don't seem to have happened at all. Yet a bigger crew of cowhands got jumped and killed. Have you ever had the feeling you're missing something?"

The clerk said not since he'd divorced his cheating wife. So they parted friendly and Longarm went to see if he could find John Miles. He owed the agent the common courtesy of informing him he'd just gotten his housekeeper murdered.

Miles wasn't in any of the few saloons along the main street. That left the local parlor houses or the summer skating rink. So, even though Miles was sending sweet-talk telegrams to his woman, Longarm decided to try the skating rink first. He'd go out of *his* way to look at an elephant, too.

As he approached the big, barnlike building the air around him tingled with an odd tinny rumble that reminded him of a cotton mill running off-key more than anything else he could think of.

Above the barn-door entrance a freshly painted sign read, "FORT RENO SUMMER SKATING PARLOR. Genuine Winslow Patent Vineyard Brand Summer Skates. Affording

Moral Uplift, Mental Acuity & The Practice of Physical Grace to the Ladies and Gents of this Fair Metropolis!"

A red-faced gent sporting a diamond or at least a good paste tiepin and a two-bit cigar presided over the stand-up ticket counter by the entrance. A pasteboard sign thumb-tacked to the front of the counter read, "Firearms, Liquor or Tobacco, smoked or chawed, not allowed on the summer rink. Patrons will refrain from pushing one another down, and lewd laughter aimed at the skating skills of the weaker sex is strictly uncalled for!"

Longarm nodded to the gent behind the counter and asked how much it cost to get in. The gent asked, "You aim to skate or just look, pard?"

Longarm said, "I'd best start with just looking. Matter of fact, I'm mostly looking for a pal of mine. You know John Miles, the Indian agent?"

The other man smiled. "Sure do. You come to the right place. You'll find him inside, just looking, too. Sometimes, when a graceful she-male ain't so graceful, you'd be sur-prised what a sharp-eyed cuss can see. Looking will cost you ten cents. Skating runs two bits an hour."

Longarm said that sounded fair and bought a looking ticket. As he pocketed his change, he couldn't help saying, "No offense, but ain't this a sort of unusual place to build a skating rink, summer *or* winter style? I should figure you'd do more business farther east, where there's more folk as cotton to newfangled notions."

The ticket seller frowned and said, "You're right as rain, cowboy. It's hell getting a man in Texas heels to try summer skating. But, you see, we're at war."

"Say again? I never heard of a summer skating war, or even a winter one, and I read the papers regular."

The older man explained, "It's a war between Free Enter-prise and the Skating Trust. On the glorious sixth of January, this very year, the notorious Plimton Patent, which had

99

hitherto kept the summer skate a monopoly for the exclusive use of the idle rich, run out. So, thanks to the self-sacrificing genius of Horace Bigelow, who thunk up hardwood ponds for summer skating but couldn't get a patent on 'em, and to the Yankee ingenuity of Sam'l Winslow, who now makes summer skates the working class can at least afford—"

Longarm cut in with a laugh. "I only asked what time it was, not how you build a clock. All you just said must be interesting as hell to anyone going in the summer skating business. But you still ain't answered how come you done so way the hell out here in the Indian Nation."

The older man grimaced. "Had to. That infernal James Plimton, who holds the original patent, is raising a cuss in the courts back East. There's no way in hell he can win, of course. His damn fool patent on ball-bearing wheels expired last winter, like I said. But meanwhile his trust is slapping injunctions pending the outcome of his case in the Supreme Court on ever'body trying to make an honest dollar with Winslow's cheaper skates."

Longarm nodded in sudden understanding and then, wondering why he was working his brain on anything that silly, wished the ticket seller luck in his quest for simple justice and went on inside.

The cavernous interior was mostly filled with a big hardwood dance floor, or in this case skating rink, but the results still resembled a barn dance, speeded up just plain silly. Somewhere in the gloom a fiddle played a reel as out on the hardwood folks reeled about on the bitty little four-wheeled wagons strapped to their feet. There were more gals than men skating out there at the moment. That didn't surprise Longarm much. He couldn't think why in thunder any grown man would want to look so foolish.

Most of the gents on the floor were soldiers from the nearby post. Enlisted men away from home would do most anything to meet a gal. The gals looked town or country, depending on how they were dressed. All of them showed more ankle than usual, taking the corners in a sassy way that made their skirts billow. Here and there in the swirling crowd he noticed a gal with her skirts cut really Rainy Susie, at least a quarter of the way up her shins. They seemed to skate better than the more sedate customers. He figured they were likely townee whores. Fancy gals had more time to kill than housewives during the hours most men were at work. A mousy little gal in a sunbonnet started to fall and one of the fancy gals caught her and steered her over to the handrail around the rink. So she was likely a good-hearted whore.

The little nester gal didn't seem upset by being forced to socialize with such a painted short-skirted gal, though. Maybe the preacher men were right, Longarm mused. Maybe such modern notions *did* encourage the younger folk to let their standards down.

Along the walls, outside the guard rails, more sensible albeit likely dirty-minded gents sat watching the scandalous proceedings from hardwood benches. Longarm spotted John Miles and worked his way over to him. He sat down by the Indian agent just as a gal lost her balance and went flat on her back, legs spread and aimed their way. Miles said, "Hot damn! Did you see that? She's got her hem down now, but for a minute, there . . ."

Longarm stared casually at the red-faced townee gal as two of the fresh-looking ones helped her to her skated feet again. He said, "She was wearing pantaloons, Johnny. I wonder how come them whores are so neighborly here."

Miles laughed. "They ain't whores, you fool. They's instructor gals. Don't know if they wear drawers under them Rainy Susies or not. They *never* fall down. What brings you here? Was I wrong about Funny Eyes?"

"First tell me how you figured she'd be willing, Johnny. I got reasons for asking."

101

The Indian agent sighed and said, "I never, if that's what you're asking. But I'll tell you man to man, it's been getting hard as hell to behave myself with that sassy Osage gal. I may look old and ugly to you, but I got natural cravings, and my old woman ain't been in a position to comfort me for a spell, now. Few nights ago that Osage gal as much as said right out she was feeling lonesome in bed alone, too. But a man would be a total lunatic to mess with his housekeeper when his wife's likely to show up any minute. So I thought, knowing you, you'd be willing to help the poor little squaw out, Longarm. Oh, Jesus, look at that one in the calico skirts! She ain't got a stitch on under it!"

"Can we talk about Funny Eyes some more, Johnny?"

"I wish you wouldn't, Longarm. One thing that's kept me pure, so far, was not being sure she really wanted it. If you tell me she *is* willing, and then ride off and leave me at her mercy..."

"You don't have to worry about that. She's dead."

Longarm had put it brutally on purpose, to see how the Indian agent's eyes read. They read surprised and confused as Miles asked, "Dead? How in the hell did she get dead? She was alive and horny as hell when I sent her out after you this very day!"

Longarm told him what had happened, in truth, then gave him his official version, and Miles agreed that it sounded nicer. He sighed and said, "Well, all we can do now is put her in a box with plenty of rock salt and ship her to the Osage agency."

Longarm explained how the Cheyenne women had agreed to bury her Indian-style. Miles swore. "Damn, I wish you hadn't let them do that, Longarm. The B.I.A. regulations call for us to plant 'em sanitary, underground. But if the squaws are already keening over her it'd cost me more trouble than it's worth to make 'em give her back. So we'd best just not mention the matter at all on the books. She wasn't registered with me as a ward, anyways."

"I got to report the murder of a lady on federal property, Johnny."

"I know. But B.I.A. just now gave the case to *you*, total! I'll answer if Washington ever asks question one about her. But I sure don't mean to *volunteer* I let 'em stick another Indian up in the sky."

Longarm frowned. "They said they'd dispose of her remains Osage style, Johnny."

"Sure they will, damn it. Cheyenne are Plains Indians. Osage are Plains Indians. It won't strain their brains to platform her like all infernal Plains Indians are wont to, when we ain't watching. I don't reckon it hurt, back in the Shining Times, when bodies got platformed here and there, across wide-open and mostly uninhabited country. But the B.I.A. ain't being mean for no reason when it forbids platforming on a *reservation*, Longarm. There's a sensible limit to how many Indians one can leave up in the sky, unembalmed, in a limited area."

Longarm sighed and said, "You're right. I was too upset about her murder to consider what they meant when they said they'd bury her for us. I just plain forgot that custom of wrapping dead folk in blankets and cradling 'em in a sort of eagle's nest on painted poles. But maybe after they're done, we can go find her with a buckboard and sort of plant her right."

Miles shook his head. "Not soon enough to matter much. They'll keep a vigil around her sky grave till the corpse stops dripping. They figure once all the juices has oozed out and the smell fades away the soul's at peace with Old Woman. Until then we can't get at her without a fuss and, after, it don't matter, sanitary-wise. I know where they'll carry her. There's a mess of old dry bones getting drier all the time in a cottonwood grove, way downwind of the agency buildings, thank God. Ever' now and again they

103

sneaks another one up in the treetops on me, there. It's best not to inquire too closely into such matters, if they're otherwise well-behaved. The old ones fear that when folk get buried white, they have to go to the white man's heaven. They must not picture it the same as us."

Longarm said, "Well, I hope Funny Eyes got to *some* sort of heaven, and I still have to put her killer in *hell!* I can't see him skating around out there on bitty wheels, so I'd best look elsewhere. Now that I'm here, serious, I'd better check out my own Winchester and McClellan, along with my possibles. If I leave the saddle, bridle, and gun I borrowed from your agency at the livery, can you get 'em back all right, Johnny?"

"Sure. Where will you be headed next, though, if not to the agency some more?"

"I'll likely get back out there a little after sundown. I said I would. But I mean to poke about some here in town while the daylight holds. We'll talk about what I find out here after I find something out. Right now I'm stuck with more questions than answers."

He rose to work his way out. Behind him, Miles and the others seated at the same vantage point gasped collectively as some gal out on the floor gasped, "Oh, oh, oh dear!" with her bare rump likely full of splinters.

He didn't look back. He'd seen gals naked before, and it only made a grown man uncomfortable to stare at one he couldn't get at.

Nearer the entrance, a gal with flaming red hair and her ass barely covered with the shortest skirt he'd seen so far that day skated up alongside him and asked, "Leaving so soon, cowboy? What's the matter? Are you chicken?"

He smiled at her. Any man would have. Then he said, "I ain't a cowboy. Ain't a chicken, neither. Just got better things to do right now."

"You look athletic-natured, handsome. I'll bet I could have you skating like an expert in no time."

"Ain't got time this time, ma'am. But in case I go loco and come back to take you up on such a kind offer, I'm Custis Long."

She dimpled. "Howdy, Custis Long. I answer to Texas Trixie. I don't mean to brag, but I skate better than any gal west of the Big Muddy. Likely east of it, too. But, like I said, I don't mean to brag."

He laughed. "I seen you twirling on one skate out there before, Texas Trixie. How much do you charge? For skating lessons, I mean."

She laughed boldly and said, "I don't charge nothing for any kind of lessons. I'm part owner of this rink, so it's in my own interest to teach as many people to skate as I can, free. You've no idea how hard it is to get cowboys and Indians on skates. Besides, you look tough. Are you tough, Custis?"

"I don't get called a sissy often, Texas Trixie. But, no offense, I don't think a man has to be tough to summer skate. I see *gals* out there I'm sure I could lick, and some are skating right well."

She sighed and said, "Yes, but not many of them figure to stand up to real trouble when it comes, and...Never mind, we'll teach you to skate when you come back, Custis."

He stopped. She grabbed the rail between them to swing around and face him, with her boldly thrust pelvis against it, aimed at his. "Before I say I'll be back or not, Texas Trixie, just what sort of trouble are you expecting?" he asked.

"They may not even come. By the way, didn't you read the sign out front covering that gun your frock coat isn't covering so well?"

He nodded. "I ain't drinking or chawing, so two out of

three ain't bad. Tell me something, Texas Trixie, did you get so interested in me before or after you noticed I was packing hardware?"

She said, "I'll be the judge of how interested I am or not after I see how well you skate. Are you law or trouble?"

"I ain't trouble to those who don't trouble me. If you folk are having trouble with someone else, you'd best stop dropping hints, temptations, or whatever, and spell it out, Texas Trixie. Like I said, I got other chores to tend, and the day's about shot."

She nodded. "We're expecting toughs from the Skating Trust. So far they haven't busted up any free-agent rinks this far west, but we got a wire they just hit one in Little Rock, and we're on the same rail line. My partner, Sandy, just put out a Hey Rube. But we fear we may need our own muscles sooner than any they can get here."

He nodded and said, "So that's why you're flirting with the only tall gent in the place packing a gun." It was a statement rather than a question. She just looked embarrassed as he added, "You know it costs more than a free skating lesson to hire a professional thug. But I thank you for considering me such a big, dumb fool."

"Then you won't be coming back?" she sighed hopelessly.

He leaned across the rail, took her soft chin in his hands, and kissed her smack on the lips, albeit gentle and just funning, before he said, "I wouldn't miss it for the world. But if I can't get back before the fight starts, you'll just have to start without me. Who's Sandy, the heavy-set gent out front?"

She said, "My God, you...you kissed me in front of God and everybody!"

"Most of the others is looking up gals' skirts, and you still ain't answered my question."

She laughed, despite her attempt to look outraged, and said, "Sandy is another girl, like me, and remember, I saw you first. Old Spud Randal, out front, just works for us. I fear he won't be much use in any kind of fight. Are you sure we can count on you getting back in time, dear?"

"We'd best stick with 'Custis' till I see. The next train from the East won't arrive this side of midnight. So just you all keep skating and . . . Oh, what's your closing time?"

"We stay open till nobody wants to skate no more. That's usually about ten or so, when the herds ain't in town. But who's to say they can't set fire to a *closed* summer skating parlor? That's what they done in Saint Joe, you know."

He said he hadn't known that, but that he'd keep it in mind. Then he left, got his gear from the baggage room at the depot, and lugged it to the livery. He saddled the borrowed Indian pony right as the Indian stable boy informed him he'd seen neither hide nor hair of a rider packing an express rifle on any color horse. Longarm tipped him generously again, anyway, and mounted up to leave.

He stopped next at the local marshal's office. He knew as soon as he stepped inside why the skating-rink gals hadn't thought to call in the local law if they were expecting trouble. A skinny old cuss at least a hundred years of age was dozing in a swivel chair with his boots up on the desk. Longarm coughed politely, and when the old man didn't even open one eye, left without disturbing him further. Busting up skating rinks was no doubt against *some* damned law or another. So someone would have to try to prevent it, and Longarm was apparently the only sworn peace officer in town who might be able to.

But the troubles of Texas Trixie and Sandy were the least of his worries at the moment. So he headed on out to the army post, casting a longer shadow across the straw stubble than he had riding in. He'd told Willy May he'd screw her

107

good around sundown. It didn't look as if he was going to make it. But, as he recalled, old Willy May screwed good at any time of day or night.

They'd sounded Retreat and the flag was down when he got to the army post. But the sun was still up—barely—and, since the army supped early, he found the officers mostly drinking dessert at their club across from the head-quarters building.

One of them was the same young lieutenant he'd met earlier that day at the agency. He seemed glad to see Long-arm, too. He bought him a drink and told a sort of snotty-looking major, bellied up with them, "Longarm, here, agrees it made no sense to search further for those renegades, once our Pawnee let us down."

That hadn't been exactly the way the conversation had gone. But Longarm nodded anyway and said, "Some day, if they ever get that flying machine of the Smithsonian professors to work, Indians won't be able to hide so good in a draw less'n a mile away. Meanwhile, they could be most anywhere, on the prod and led by a better-than-average war chief. So if I was in charge I wouldn't be looking for 'em with less than a full brigade."

The major snorted, "Good God, a full brigade to fight a handful of old ragged-ass Cheyenne?"

Longarm picked up his free drink as he said, "Not to fight 'em. To *find* 'em. The prairie's firmed up again. Raining Stars didn't leave sign for your Pawnee to read even riding over it softer. They ain't pitching their tipis. They're eating their grub cold. So your only chance would be big, widespread cavalry sweeps to the southwest. That way you might at least trip over 'em, if they ain't moving fast. But they likely are. They're all mounted adults, running scared and careful, without stopping to make camp or even cut wires. So by now they're likely in the Staked Plains, holed

108

up in some unmapped canyon, waiting with guns cocked for what happens next."

The major grimaced and said, "Our jurisdiction doesn't extend that far west. We have wired the Tenth Cav. They say they've seen no sign of any unreconstructed Indians down that way."

Longarm tasted his rye. It wasn't Maryland, but it was good. "Well, if Raining Stars ain't looking for trouble, the Tenth won't likely get any from him," he said. "I rode over here on more pressing matters. Something funny is going on, over to the Cheyenne agency, and I don't see it as the work of the runaway band. Have any of your troopers been sniped at by a double-barrel express rifle lately?"

Both officers looked blank. Longarm nodded. "That's what I was afraid of. It's personal. Not some nut riding around shooting at just anybody."

He brought them up-to-date, keeping the part about the late Funny Eyes pure, and added, "So what we got is a killer who just don't want me looking for Raining Stars, who's long gone and miles from here by now, or maybe something *else* neither the whites nor the Indians at the Fort Reno agency have noticed up to now."

"How do you know nobody has?" asked the young lieutenant.

Longarm took another sip of rye. "If anyone over there does, they're too sneaky to tell me about it. I keep coming back to the junior agent, Hutchins, and his wife, as I run around in circles. Don't it strike you odd that only one white family on the reserve was even *informed* Raining Stars was set to jump, let alone harmed in any way?"

The major growled, "I'm glad to see we agree on some things, after all. I think it's fishy as hell. I thought it was sort of fishy when Dull Knife jumped the reserve a while back. The same John D. Miles was the agent in charge at that time, too, and they didn't harm a hair on his head, as I recall!"

Longarm finished the drink and put the glass down hard. He shook his head. "We're starting to disagree some more, Major. I've heard tell of crooked Indian agents. I've put more than one in jail in my time. But the reason Dull Knife didn't take Johnny Miles's hair with him as *he* left for home was that Miles treats Indians fair and they know it. The reason we keep licking the poor bastards is that they don't look at war like we do. Let Indians go on the warpath, and white men fixing to kill each other over the same woman will drop everything to fight Indians side by side. But Indians see warfare more personal. They concentrate on killing whites they don't like, or, at worst, whites they don't know. They hardly ever turn on any white who's been decent to 'em in the past, the poor dumb bastards. I met a couple of buffalo hunters a few years ago. They'd been camped near the Little Bighorn in the summer of seventy-six."

"Jesus, the time Custer caught it?"

"Yep, not more'n a day's ride from where these old boys was drying pegged-out hides. Anyways, as they were setting there, a band of thirty-odd Lakota rode into their camp, painted for war. So naturally them old white boys figured they could be in trouble. But, as it turned out, one of the Lakota in the band knew one of the buffalo hunters, friendly. They'd hunted and squawed together a few winters past, and the white boy had shared gunpowder and tobacco with the painted cuss. So he told his Lakota pals these particular white boys was Good Hearts. They smoked on it and rode on, to hit the Seventh Cav the next day. Does that answer your question about Johnny Miles's hair?"

The junior officer nodded. The major looked unconvinced. So Longarm added, "Miles was back East when Raining Stars and his band lit out. Young Hutchins, *not* Miles, was keeping the books, and the books say *nobody*

110

was screwing the Indians. So I have spoken on that subject. Next subjects, in order of urgency, are, how do I find Doc McUlric around here, and do they sell civilians drinks at this officers' club?"

The friendly young lieutenant laughed. "You can't buy drinks here, but I can. Bartender? See that this unkempt civilian gets all he wants to drink, and put it on my bill." Then he told Longarm, "That Indian agency medic should be over at the dispensary still. I'll send a runner for him."

Longarm shook his head. "I'd best go over myself, but I sure hope your barkeep has a good memory for civilian faces. I'll be back soon."

He went out, asked directions, and crossed the parade to the white frame building sick soldiers were supposed to report to.

Doc McUlric, filling in for the regular army surgeon whether he wanted to or not, turned out to be a gray, bearish man Longarm took a liking to on sight. The doc had his own snakebite remedy in a desk drawer and so could offer Longarm more than a seat as the deputy brought him up-to-date on the doings at the agency. Then he sipped McUlric's malt liquor some more and said, "What I really wanted to talk to you about was that poor bastard you got strapped down at the agency, Doc. Is it safe to assume he must have been a mite high-strung even before them Indians rode off with his horse and woman? Nurse Willy May has him so doped up I can't get any sense out of him. She says them was your instructions."

McUlric nodded. "They were. Frankly, if we can't get him to snap out of it soon, I'll have to send him off to an asylum. A certain amount of hysteria is to be expected, when one considers what the Indians have no doubt done to the poor girl by now. But, yes, Bill Hutchins has been overreacting to his misfortunes. Most men in his position would have stopped weeping and wailing and just gone out

111

to kill some Indians by now. He's cracked completely. Doubt he'll recover soon. You're right about him having been tense to begin with."

"You knew him, of course, before it happened?"

"Of course. Ever since he and his wife, Helen, arrived. Six months or more ago, I think. He didn't make a very favorable impression on me, as a man. As a medical man, I suspected he might be a borderline case."

"Borderline of what, Doc?"

"I'd better choose my words carefully, Longarm. You see, effeminate manners don't always mean a man's a . . . well . . . pervert."

"Don't shilly-shally, Doc. Was he a sissy or wasn't he?"

"He was married to a rather attractive woman, if that's what you mean. They seemed to get along well enough. So he must have been doing *something* right. But, well, have you ever met a boy who just naturally seemed to get his hat thrown up on roofs by all the other boys?"

"In other words, we're talking about a plain old sissy, not a disgusting one. Did the Indians bully him, Doc?"

"Not as far as I could see. They tend to think all white men are sort of sissy. Must confuse hell out of them to be on reservations now. I guess Hutchins got along well enough with the wards left in his charge by Miles. If he was a mite more generous on rations day, *that* certainly gave them no call to be mad at him, at least."

"Maybe they was just mad at his wife, since he's still got all his hair, even sobbing to himself in bed. What was *she* like, Doc?"

McUlric shrugged and said, "Young, pretty, soft, and spoiled, but not nasty about it. She obviously didn't like it out here, and she seemed a bit afraid of the Indians. I can't see her insulting or mistreating them, if that's what you mean. She kept mostly to herself. Stayed in the house a lot, save on rations day, when she helped her husband hand out

112

the cash allowances and such. They had Indian help actually cutting up the sides of beef and hefting the flour sacks, of course."

"Ever hear her arguing with any of the Cheyenne as to what was due 'em?"

"Lord, no. As I said, if anything they were overgenerous. They reminded me of two lost babes in the wood, surrounded by growling red ogres they wanted to please real bad."

"You say she was pretty. At least one Indian I talked to says she was ugly and too skinny," Longarm observed.

McUlric chuckled. "One of the reasons our squaw men get what they consider the best-looking squaws is that our views on female beauty don't agree. Helen Hutchins is, or *was,* a nice-looking willowy blonde, by our standards. Obviously Raining Stars admired her looks, too, don't you think?"

Longarm took out a cheroot to inhale with the malt liquor lest it get the best of him. "Don't know what to think, Doc," he said. "I've noticed Cheyenne favor big, strong, moon-faced gals, and the last time I met up with Raining Stars he looked too old and beat to be interested much in *any* kind of gal. But there's no accounting for tastes. Does anybody have a picture of old Helen, in case I stumble over a skinny blonde in an Indian camp someday?"

McUlric said he was sure there'd be tintypes of her in the Hutchinses' quarters, adding that neither the Indians nor anyone else had trifled with their belongings since the tragedy. So Longarm set that aside and said, "Let's talk about the other whites who got unlucky with the band, Doc. Who signed their death certificates? You?"

McUlric grimaced. "Had to. Nobody else wanted to examine their bodies. They were messed up pretty good, and starting to decompose."

He opened a drawer and took out a stack of paper-backed

113

photographs, adding, "I had these taken before I cut 'em open. You can see how they'd started to darken by the time they were found."

Longarm's tobacco smoke started tasting sort of vile as he forced himself to examine the close-up photographs of some mighty dead-looking faces. He said, "I can see somebody surely dented *this* one's skull. War club?"

"Has to be. A baseball bat or a two-by-four wouldn't have left the same rounded indentations. They weren't scalped, though. That one missing most of his hair and some of his face was gnawed by coyotes. The tooth marks on the skull don't show so good in that picture, but..."

"I'll take your word you got a better look at 'em." Longarm went on, "You say you autopsied 'em anyways, Doc. How come? Ain't it sort of obvious they got killed by warclub strokes?"

McUlric pursed his lips and said, "I'm paid to do a thorough job, so I looked for bullets as well as water in the lungs. Found neither."

Longarm blinked in sudden interest and asked, "You feared they'd died of *drowning*, Doc?"

"Had to at least consider it. They had been camped on low ground during an unexpected summer squall. The bodies could have been mutilated by passing sullen Indians afterwards."

"Were they?"

"No. We don't perform autopsies just to mess bodies up. We like to know the cause of death before we sign for it. They were killed by repeated blows on the head. Dead brains don't bleed internally. So the flood silt some of their clothes were stained with had nothing to do with their deaths, and some of them didn't get touched by the running water in the draw at all. It was a red herring, but it pays to make sure."

Longarm grinned. "It fixes the time of death better, too!

You're a good doc, Doc. You just restored the honor of some no-doubt chagrined Pawnee scouts, too. I'd best go tell the army how it works."

They shook on it and he crossed over to rejoin his friendly lieutenant and not-so-friendly major at the officers' club. As he bellied up to the bar with them again the barkeep slid another tumbler of rye his way. Longarm sipped just enough to be polite without risking a fall from his pony outside in the near future and said, "Raining Stars jumped the reserve before that big storm, not during it, like folk thought."

The major asked, "Oh, who says so?"

Longarm said, "The prairie. If the Indians hit them cowhands in the draw just before the storm, they'd have come and gone across earth baked hard as 'dobe. Then the rain messed up any sign they left in the sandy draw, afoot *or* ahorse. Then the floodwaters coming after the Cheyenne was long gone complicated things even more by shifting at least some of the bodies about and making 'em spoil faster when the sun come out again. The reason your scouts couldn't cut no trail out of there was an act of nature, not weak Pawnee eyes."

The major objected, "If they left even earlier than we were told, then by now they're even farther away than we thought, damn it!"

Longarm said, "I know. With every foot- or hoofprint they may have left on bare ground erased forever by the Thunder Bird. So how come some damned body is worried about me tracking 'em at *this* late date?"

The junior officer tried helpfully, "What if your mysterious bushwhacker's trying to cover some *other* crime, Longarm?"

"First thing I thought of. But what's left to cover? The only breach of B.I.A. regulations I know of in these parts consists of a poor old loco Indian taking French leave and, by now, likely getting away with it, if he behaves himself

115

till he just dies of old age, which can't take all that long. Him and his ragged-ass old sidekicks seemed to have cooled off from their first boyish enthusiasm, since they ain't hit nobody else, recent. They'll probably just stay as far away from any whites as they can get now, trying to live on what game's left in the Staked Plains."

"They owe us for that white girl and those white cowhands," the major objected, "and I still don't see why you're so sure they headed for the Staked Plains, Longarm."

Longarm said, "There's no place else they could hope to last long enough to matter, and so far we ain't found 'em dead *or* alive. The country's too settled in every other direction to slip through so sneaky. Dull Knife found that out when he jumped this same reserve, and it was more open, then. There's no place closer than the Staked Plains a South Cheyenne could hope to survive without a permit from the Great White Father."

"Why stop at the Staked Plains?" the major sniffed. "Why not ride on to Mexico or Apacheria, where we'd *never* find them?"

Longarm sniffed right back and said, "They may act that dumb. If they do, you're right, and nobody will ever find 'em. All the other good Indian and outlaw country's *took*, by Indians or outlaws who'd make mincemeat out of poor old Raining Stars and his few old braves. Forget Raining Stars. He's gone. But some other pest keeps pegging shots at me, and I have to figure out why, so's I can go home and let *you* boys worry about rounding up tired, half-starved Indians."

As he put down his glass and started for the door, the young lieutenant asked where he was going. So Longarm said, "Out to *look* for the son of a bitch, of course. I doubt like hell he's stationed on this post!"

Chapter 8

Longarm circled wide across rolling and hopefully unin-habited prairie to approach the Indian agency from an angle someone with an express rifle might not be set up for. He reined in now and again to wait for anyone following him with or without murderous intent. The sun was down but the moon was up by now. So, while the shadows were black enough for hiding, a gent reined in invisible could see pretty good across the silvery moonlit grass he'd just ridden.

This far from town, and woodcutters from either the army post or the agency, the draws were lined with more sub-stantial timber. Some of the trees grew as high as the rims of the lower draws. But naturally the winter wolf winds saw they grew no higher. So, from a rise, it looked like flat, open prairie all around. It was exactly the kind of country the more truculent Plains Indians had favored in the wild old Shining Times. But a white man who knew the sneaky lay of the land could use it for easy ambush himself any old time.

Because he'd circled, Longarm wasn't expecting anyone to lay for him ahead. His laying for anyone following him didn't seem to be panning out either, and by now poor Willy May would be getting impatient. So he decided just to ride on in, and the hell with it.

He topped a rise and reined in again, looking ahead, not back, as the night breeze throbbed like a beating heart in his ears. He clucked his buckskin on at a walk and, next rise, he could tell it was a medicine drum making all that racket. Closer in, sad, chanting she-male voices added to the dismal atmosphere. He told his mount, "If we're not careful we'll find ourselves uninvited guests at an old-fashioned Indian funeral. We'd best swing wide, Buck."

They did, moving down into a cottonwood-groved draw. The buckskin mare balked at going farther, or tried to. Longarm glanced up at the moonlight slanting spookily through the ink-black branches above and heeled her flanks harder, saying, "I smell the breath of Mr. Death, too. But it can't be helped, Buck. To get to the other side, and Willy May, we got to cross through this valley of mortality."

The buckskin didn't like it, but she moved on. Longarm didn't like it much either. He couldn't help noticing what looked like big birds' nests here and there in the trees above. He knew it smelled worse to his mount down here than it did to him. Poor little Funny Eyes hadn't been dead long enough to stink and apparently nobody else had been planted in the sky here recently. The still air down out of the wind smelled, to him, like Shiloh had the time he'd passed through a second time, a year after the battle. Stale death smelled sort of sour and cobwebby. A human nose could miss it entirely unless, knowing he was passing through its shadow, he sniffed hard. Longarm prefered to breathe shallow, through his mouth, on old battlefields and outdoor burial grounds. He was only interested in one particular body in this neck of the woods, and he didn't really want to smell what Funny Eyes figured to smell like in a day or so.

They'd made it more than halfway to the other side of the cottonwoods when the buckskin shied at something white on the ground ahead. Longarm steadied her and said, "I see it, Buck. It's just an old skull that fell out of a tree a long time ago. When the wind blows, the cradle will rock, see?"

He grimaced as he couldn't help noting other fallen objects all around between the trees by the moonlight. Most were baskets, dried-out rat-chawed medicine bags, pipes, and such. But here and there a thighbone, a rib, or another skull lay scattered across the ground. He told his mount, "Let's get out of here, Buck. I've always found funeral parlors sort of depressing, but this is ridiculous!"

They went up the far slope and Longarm inhaled clean prairie wind again with considerable relief. He tried to keep an open mind, and most Indians found him more understanding than most other whites. So he knew Native Americans had lots of good notions, or at least notions that made sense once you tried to understand them. But he just couldn't hold with some of their views on sanitation. He knew a body buried six feet down got just as messy, or even more so, since he'd had to exhume a few for evidence in his time. But like their somewhat casual notions of housecleaning, sky burials only worked decent when a band kept moving on in mostly empty country. A tipi ring inhabited by nomadic hunters smelled no worse, and sometimes better, than a white slum. But if the Great White Father expected Mister Lo to stay put on limited land, something was going to have to give. If the High Plains Nations didn't learn to live more white, like the Cherokee, Osage, and such to the east, they were simply going to die out from the white man's bugs they picked up along with his rations and allowances. Convincing them that cholera and consumption were the results of crowded, messy living and not the work of evil spirits could be a chore, though. He didn't envy Willy May her job as reservation nurse.

He grinned and told his mount, "Speaking of old Willy May, what in the hell are we poking along out here on the prairie for when she's waiting for us—or me, at least—at the dispensary?"

He rode in the rest of the way at a lope. When he reined in near the back door, sure enough, Willy May was standing there, with the lamplight from behind her shining scandalously through her thin cotton kimono.

He tethered the buckskin to the water pump out back and pumped a handy bucket of water for her before joining Willy May in the doorway and kicking the door shut with a boot heel as he took her in his arms.

She sobbed, "Oh, I was so afraid you'd met another gal, Custis!"

He had, but he soothed, "Ain't a gal as pretty as you in the Indian Nation, honey. But let go a minute, will you? I'd like to see if Hutchins is in better condition to talk before I give you my undivided attention."

"Damn it, he's under sedation on doctor's orders and I'm hot as a two-dollar pistol!"

He said, "Me, too. But we got till eleven or later. I just talked to your Doc McUlric. He's all right. Come on, let's find out if Hutchins has to be shipped to the funny farm, or if he wants to act like a man for a change."

She followed him down the hall, clucking like a hen in heat, and he found the junior agent in the dark. He struck a match, lit the candle on the bed table, and asked Willy May if a nightlight might not be easier on her patient's nerves. She said, "Waking up in a burning building can make *me* nervous, too!" and Longarm had to allow that made sense.

He pulled up the same bentwood chair and, since the nurse had already shown him how, slapped Hutchins at least semi-conscious. He must not have been as full of dope, now. His eyes not only opened but looked almost in focus as he asked Longarm if they'd found his wife yet.

"We need your help, old son," Longarm told him. "For openers I'd like to see a picture of your woman. You got one handy?"

"On my desk, in our quarters," Hutchins said. "I always keep her tintype before me as I work, along with Mamma's."

"Well, boys is supposed to be fond of their mothers. I

120

reckon I can figure out which one's the younger of the two. You got a key to your quarters?"

"In my pants, if I knew where my pants were. Why am I strapped down like this? *I* haven't done anything wrong! It's the Indians! I knew they hated us! Helen knew it, too. She begged me over and over to send her back East, but I insisted like a fool they'd get used to us, and . . . Oh, God, what if they've raped her?"

"They might not," Longarm soothed, not really sure one way or the other, but not wanting to point out the obvious alternative. "I know old Raining Stars," he went on. "He didn't strike me as a man who hated without good reason. So tell me why you think him and his were so down on you, Hutchins."

The weakling in the bed sobbed, "I don't know why they hated us. They just did. You could see it in their eyes. They tried to hide it. But it's not true Indians have poker faces. Mamma used to look at me that same way when I was bad, when I was little. But, damn it, I didn't *do* anything bad out here. I haven't been bad since I got married, like Mamma said I should!"

Longarm glanced up at the nurse standing at the foot of the bed. Willy May nodded thoughtfully. But what a no-doubt stern mother had caught a little sissy boy doing out behind the barn had little bearing on the current situation, save for the fact that a weak sister with a guilty conscience pounded into him could likely read more into casual glances than most might. He saw that Hutchins was dozing off again, so he shook him awake and said, "Not yet, old son. You say your woman thought the Indians were mad at her, too. I'll tell you true that some remember her as sort of snooty. So I want you to think hard before you answer. Did your Helen ever have actual words with Raining Stars or anyone from his band?"

Hutchins shook his head to clear it and muttered, "No.

121

If anything, she went out of her way to be nice to all of them. More than once, when we went over the books together, we saw that she'd paid out twice for the same Indian dependent. They have such funny names, and only the family heads have serial numbers. But Helen said, and I agreed, that it was better to err on the safe side with such savage people."

Longarm grimaced and said, "Well, I've heard of agents getting the figures wrong, but seldom in the Indians' favor. I'd say killing the golden goose would be dumb as hell, even for a man given to big medicine visions."

"My God, do you mean they may have *killed* Helen?"

"Of course not," Longarm lied. "But let's study medicine, Indian style. Bear with me as I pontificate on it, some, so's you'll follow my drift better before answering. Cheyenne have Algonquin notions of religion, which is something like our own, in ways, and a heap different in others. Our missionaries ain't always careful when they write things down. They're sort of influenced by their own notions. So it ain't true that Manitou translates exactly as Great Spirit, or the Lord, and what they tend to think of as the Wendigo, or devil, ain't exactly our gent with horns and a tail. They're both what we translate as medicine, incarnate or polarized. We call it medicine because it includes healing, sickness, and so forth. But power, magic, or unusual *luck* would be closer to what the Indians really mean. They set great store by *omens* they read as ... well ... medicine, good or bad."

At the foot of the bed, Willy May said, "He isn't following you, honey. I can't, and I'm wide awake. Let's go make good medicine of our own."

Longarm shook his head. "Look, Hutchins, Plains Indians read medicine or magic into all sorts of unusual happenings. A white buffalo has to mean something, since it don't happen every hunt. Many a lunatic has been spared a scalping because it ain't usual to meet a prospective victim

122

who just acts silly when he should be fighting or at least running. A while back an albino baby was born to the Mandan Nation. We called him Big White and treated him as a chief because the Mandan did, too. In point of fact he was a big, pale half-wit. But to the Mandan he'd been touched by big medicine, so he had to be important. Indians have also been known to kill otherwise harmless enough folk whose unusual traits struck some medicine man or spirit dreamer as *Wendigo,* or *bad* medicine. So think hard and tell me if there was anything unusual about your wife, aside from her being white and sort of shy. Was she sort of cock-eyed? Did she have a facial tic, or a habit of walking backwards now and again? Walking backwards can get you in a lot of trouble. You see, Spirit Bears pretending to be humans do that a lot, and..."

He stopped when he saw that Hutchins had gone under again. As he rose, Willy May said, "I knew the silly girl well enough to tell you she wasn't in any way deformed or given to acting crazy in public."

Longarm said, "Where's his pants? I still want a look at her picture. It's a pain looking for people when you don't have the least notion what on earth they look like. The world is full of wispy dishwater blondes. So I can't help drawing a picture of the missing gal in my head, and that can throw a searcher way the hell off."

"God damn it, Custis, do you mean to search for her *tonight?* I thought we had an understanding about tonight, you brute!"

He smiled. "I'll be able to treat you better if I ain't trying to picture another gal I've never seen at the same time, see?"

She opened a wardrobe and got out the keys for him. "All right, get it over with, and then I'll expect you all over me, you slowpoke. Are you sure you haven't been with another gal today, Custis? I don't recall having this much trouble getting you started the last time."

He chuckled fondly, pocketed the key ring, and they walked to the rear entrance together as he sort of comforted her rear with a friendly hand. She said, "Don't do that. I don't want to waste an orgasm on thin air. Damn, I wish there was time for me to slip into my uniform and come with you. It might be fun in a strange bedroom."

He laughed and said, "I'd be back to your own by the time you could get decent, honey. Besides, I ain't sure it's decent, fornicating in another lady's bed without her permit. By the way, what did you mean about acting normal in public? Have you reason to suspect she acted crazy in *private?*"

Willy May shrugged and said, "Not really. Just a feeling. As a nurse, I'm used to having other women confide in me. I told you the trader's woman comes to me for medicine a young gal married to an old man needs to calm her nerves. She takes precautions as well, so he can't *always* act so old. But Helen Hutchins never came to this dispensary for *any* female reasons."

"Well, maybe she was just naturally healthy."

"Childless, too. And there's no drug store in town, if you get my meaning."

"Don't speak ill of the likely dead. Her sex life ain't important to the case, unless she was having the same with Indians even *before* they kidnapped her. But if she'd been fooling around that way, she'd have come to you for medical supplies for sure! Her and her husband both being fair-haired, a gal out to change her luck would likely be even more careful than most."

"Is that a crack? Are you hinting I might have an Indian lover on the side, you bastard?"

He stepped out the door, gave her a friendly feel, and said, "If you have, don't tell me about him. I'm jealous-natured. Be right back to prove it."

124

But it didn't work out quite that way. As Longarm approached the dark quarters of the junior agent's little frame house he saw by the lights in the windows of John Miles's larger place that the senior agent was back from town and, even better, too smart to sit inside a lit-up window with the curtains undrawn. He had no reason to pester Miles at the moment, so he just quietly unlocked the back door of the deserted Hutchins house and went on in.

The interior smelled musty after not being cooked in or even aired for over a week. But thanks to the late Funny Eyes, or maybe the late Helen Hutchins, everything was neatly in place. Indian kids didn't prowl empty houses as often as white kids. They considered stealing anything smaller than a horse sort of petty, and didn't believe in the same kind of haunts.

The modest quarters consisted of four rooms: a kitchen, a bath, a living room, and the bedroom Hutchins had also been using as his office, judging by a rolltop desk in one corner. Longarm grinned as he considered how downright comfortable it might be to go over one's books with a willing she-male waiting just across the room in bed for one to finish. They had *twin* beds, he noticed. But, since neither was occupied at the moment, it wasn't his problem. He'd thought Hutchins looked sort of prim.

Atop the rolltop, two gals stared primly at him when he struck a match for a better look, found a candle stub, and lit it. The window shades were drawn, so he didn't have to worry about anyone gunning him from outside as he sat down at the desk, shook out the match, and tried to decide which of the framed tintypes disapproved of him the most.

The older gal, who had to be Mamma, wore her gray or blonde hair in a severe bun. Her features were pleasant enough, but her mouth was set like she'd just caught someone jacking off in the outhouse. He smiled back at her and said, "My hands is both in plain view on this desk, ma'am."

125

She went on looking as if she didn't believe him anyway. The picture of the younger gal to her left looked mighty depressing, too. He could see now why she'd been described as attractive by whites and ugly by Indians. Whites tended to go by features. Her features were regular. But Indians tended to look at the inner features of folk more than they did the skin-deep parts, and that was one mean-hearted little gal. As a lawman, Longarm was trained to read inner character. So he said, "I'd want twin beds, shacked up with you, too, lady. Them eyes is as generous and forgiving as an Apache looking at a tied-up Mexican! It's just as well you two ain't had any kids up to now. If we get you back, and you ever do, the poor little bastards will likely get their mouths washed out with laundry soap as often as they eat dessert!"

He ignored the grim portrait, now that he'd at last fixed her missing features in his mind's eye, and started rummaging through desk drawers. But he found no B.I.A. papers. Miles had apparently carried them over to his place next door, once he got back.

Longarm stood up and was about to blow out the candle when he noticed ladder steps running up the back wall of an open closet nearer the twin beds. He moved closer and saw they led up through an open trap above the closet. He had no idea what they might have in their attic, but it was easy enough to find out, so he climbed up the ladder.

He didn't bother going all the way. For once he had his head and shoulders above the edge of the trap he could see by the moonlight filtering through the vent slats at one end that it was just a low air space under the shallow-pitched roof. There was nothing stored up there. Hutchins had probably left the trap open once summer was upon them, for ventilation.

Longarm went back down, snuffed the candle, and started

126

to leave. But then he stiffened as he heard someone messing with the back door he'd locked after him coming in. It had a catch lock that had to be opened with a key each time, and whoever wanted in was working harder with a pick.

He started to leave via the front door, then wondered why he'd want to do a dumb thing like that. So he ducked back in the bedroom and went back up the ladder all the way to lie flat on the rafters above, gun drawn, as he waited to see what happened next.

What happened next was that two people, a man and a woman, came into the bedroom, holding hands and giggling. The gal whispered, "Raise the shade, darling. I love to watch you sliding in and out of me!"

So the young Indian with her laughed and raised the back shade to flood the twin beds in moonlight as the gal—a white one—shucked her duds pronto and sprawled across it, face up, naked. She couldn't see Longarm staring down at her from what *she* could only see as the black ceiling of the nearby closet. But Longarm could see everything she had to offer, from head to toe, and he hadn't noticed, at the trading post, that the shy-acting little trader's wife had such an hourglass shape.

The Indian with her was Wetfeather. He looked about as expected, with his duds off, save for the heroic hard-on he displayed as he dropped his jeans and climbed on the bed with her. He started to mount her right off, but she said, "Wait, I want to get you nice and slickery, darling!"

Wetfeather must have wanted to get nice and slickery, too. For the next thing Longarm knew they were going sixty-nine right under him, as he wondered how in thunder he was going to get back to Willy May.

He couldn't, at the moment, and while what they were doing right under his nose was sort of interesting, he'd never considered sex a spectator sport. He wanted to *do* it, not *watch* it! For as the bawdy little trader gal betrayed her poor old husband down there, the damned old Indian was having all the fun.

Longarm could see why she'd picked that particular peace officer to give a piece to tonight. Old Wetfeather could sure move his brown rump as he laid her, spread-eagled on the bed, with her wide eyes staring right up at Longarm till he was sure she could see him. But she was just wide-eyed from getting screwed so good, apparently, for she suddenly closed 'em, bit her lower lip, and hissed, "Oh, yes! Harder, harder!"

Wetfeather stopped what he was doing and whispered, "Listen, white woman, I hope you've taken precautions. I'm not worried about your husband as much as I am my people! They'd shit if they knew I was fooling with white meat!"

She moaned, "Don't worry. I told you the nurse is a real pal. Just *do* it to me, darling! Nobody will ever know!"

That wasn't true, since Longarm was watching as the young buck came in her, hard, and rolled off, panting for breath as now, damn it, they *both* seemed to be staring right up at him!

The white gal said, "Oh, that was lovely. I can't wait to do it again."

But Wetfeather, bless him, said, "I have to get back to my post. I told you I'm on duty tonight, and Miles will have my ass if he finds out I'm not out patrolling the edges of the agency like he ordered."

"To hell with that silly old agent, darling. *I* want your ass! Oh, God, how I want it bounding betwixt my open thighs some more."

Wetfeather laughed and said, "He'll see me out of my job, sure, if I let that mysterious rifleman get close enough to do more harm. Maybe you don't take him as seriously as me because you weren't there when he spanged a slug through the backrest between me and that white lawman, Longarm."

"Pooh! Let Longarm and the other Indian lawmen worry about that silly with an express rifle. Put your own big gun in me again!"

Longarm was surely wishing Wetfeather would do *something* down there so he could get down from here. It was all he could do to keep from shouting down, "Screw her or get back to your post, you fool!"

Great minds seemed to run in the same channels. The young Indian said, "All right. Once more. But then I really have to get back to earning my pay, honey."

Suiting actions to his words, Wetfeather proceeded to hump her good. She started hammering the mattress with clenched fists as she pleaded, "Faster, faster! Fuck me wild and dirty, you savage!"

She shouldn't have said that. The Indian screwing her went cigar-store Indian and stopped. He growled, "Hey, don't call me a *savage*, you white whore! *I'm* not the one who's cheating on a husband you got drunk on purpose. I'm not the one who started this either! If you think it's a dirty thrill to fuck an Indian, get yourself another Indian!"

He withdrew from her and sat on the bed to start hauling on his jeans as she whimpered, "Don't be angry, darling. I didn't know what I was saying!"

"I did. Lots of you people think you'll find a new thrill with someone of another race. But hear me: all people are made the same. And you're not as great as you think you are."

She rolled over and tried to suck him again. He pushed her roughly away and said, "I mean what I say when I speak. I don't talk silly just to make myself hot. I have no trouble getting hot with any friendly woman. But you are not friendly. You're just dirty-minded. Go home and suck your poor old husband. You might find that an even *more* unusual thrill. We are through. I have spoken."

He got to his feet and grumped out with his Indian feet in white man's boots as she pleaded, "Wait, we have to talk!" She slipped her own clothes on, sort of, and chased him out of the room.

Longarm waited until he heard the back door slam, open, and slam again before he climbed down the ladder. He left by the front door, not wanting to stumble over anyone screwing in the back yard, and circled back to the dispensary. To say he found Willy May mad as a wet hen would have been understating her condition by a wide margin. As he joined her, the nurse said, "You . . . bastard! Don't you touch me!"

He didn't, since she was holding a bottle in one maidenly fist as they faced each other just inside her back door. But he said, "I thought that was what you wanted me to do, little darling. We've been trying to find the time since I got here."

Her kimono was open, temptingly, but her face was almost as grim as if it had been framed atop the Hutchins rolltop as she snapped, "Don't try to lie your way back into my good graces, you randy rascal! Do you think I'm so ugly I have to go seconds to a *squaw?*"

He frowned and said, "I ain't been with no squaw, re-cent." Which was the simple truth, in a way, since Funny Eyes had been dead for hours. But Willy May said, "That's a lie. I just went over to the Hutchins house in my kimono, to see what was taking you so long. Are you trying to tell me you were doing all that love moaning inside all by yourself?" Her voice went high-pitched and mocking as she mimicked, "'Faster, faster, I'm coming, darling!' Ain't it amazing how fast they pick up English, once they start screwing white men?"

Longarm grinned sheepishly and said, "Let's see how I can explain without getting others in trouble."

"Don't bother trying," Willy May sobbed. "Get *out* of

130

here, you two-timing squaw man!"

She sounded like she meant it. He cast a last wistful glance at the front of her open kimono and said, "Well, I promised to get back to town before midnight, anyway."

For some reason that made her throw the bottle at him as he ducked out the door. But she was so upset she missed by a good two inches.

Chapter 9

Longarm now had more time to kill than he'd expected, and the buckskin had been ridden hard that day. So he led her over to the Indian police station and swapped her for a black stud with white stockings and blaze.

The Indian wrangler on duty didn't want him shooting any more of the stock, so the fresh mount didn't buck once as he mounted up to ride off the agency again. The stud nickered as they took the wagon trace through a sapling grove.

Longarm reined in, put a thoughtful hand on his saddle gun, and then, as the other rider moved out in the moonlight, said, "Evening, Wetfeather. Glad to see you're a man of your word."

The young Indian asked what he was talking about. Longarm said, "I don't know. We always talk sort of odd. You and your gun would have likely said something more important had anyone come riding in the *other* way, recent. But do you mind a tip on picket riding from an old army man, even a white one?"

"You're right. You do talk funny. But I am listening."

"You don't figure to catch any mysterious night riders here on the wagon trace, old son. I just came in from the army post without using any trail at all, and I wasn't sneaking up on nobody."

"I know this is a stupid place to post a picket. But I was posted here," Wetfeather said.

132

"Well, the nice thing about standing guard dumb is that it don't hurt to go take a leak or something, if you don't overdo it. While I'm here discussing night riding with a man who knows the lay of the land in these parts better than me, I may as well mention I rode through that draw your old folk favor as a sky burial ground."

"You shouldn't have done that. Not even Indians are supposed to bother the spirits of the dead."

"I didn't steal any arrowheads or pottery. Steered clear of the old squaws keening over, or under, Funny Eyes. But tell me, how many Cheyenne have been buried, or lifted, recent over there?"

"You are wise for a white man. I thought of that, too. We all did. We looked to see if the missing white woman had been left in the sky over there. She hadn't. A couple of children and one old man have been left among the treetops since the spring thaw. Nobody else. Most of our people no longer do it. The medicine men say it's better to risk the white man's heaven than to smell so bad so close to the living. So most of my people bury their dead like you people do, now. The old ones who carried off the dead Osage girl are of the old school. But hardly any of them are left. People do not live to be so old on a reservation. I think that is why Raining Stars left. He was not a bad person. He just wanted to die free, out on the old hunting grounds."

Longarm said, "Well, with luck, he may find an acre nobody's filed a claim on or built a railroad across yet. I thought Raining Stars was a good person, too. But aside from the missing white gal, he's got them dead cowhands to account for. How do you explain that, from a religious viewpoint?"

Wetfeather shrugged. "I can't. The old chief did not share his vision with me. But maybe the white woman just went away on her own. Maybe other Indians killed those cowboys. Did anyone see Raining Stars and his band do it?"

"I'll score that for you, if you'll grant me there's no other bands running wild on the prairie in these parts this summer. The other agencies have all been counting noses since Raining Stars turned up missing. So far, all reservation Indians within miles are present and accounted for."

"Isn't it possible some band that's just never come in yet is still out there?"

"Let's not talk dumb, old son. We ain't in the Shining Times no more. The plains between here and the shining mountains are so crowded some of us old-timer *whites* are complaining about bobwire and dammed springs. The buffalo south of the transcontinental rails have been wiped out, and buffalo hardly ever commit suicide. So it's hardly likely all them buffalo hiders could have missed a leftover wild band, as they searched every hill and dale for anything tall enough to skin out. By now we know old Raining Stars has found a hidey-hole, since nobody seems to be able to find him. But to get to it, he had to ride over them cowhands, and he rode over 'em pretty good. He could have had his reasons. Some Texas riders have been known to act surly to strange Indians. Your notion the white gal could have ridden off on her own, timing it sort of confusing, works up to a point. They don't allow even thoroughbreds aboard railroad trains, so she'd have had to leave her mount in town or check him aboard a freight car, see?"

"How do you know she didn't?" the Indian asked.

Longarm started to object, then nodded. *"You're* smart, too. I'd best do just that. It's been nice talking to you, Wetfeather."

He rode on, following the wagon trace but not right on it as he looked both ways in the moonlight to see if he was alone. He seemed to be. He got to town with no further incident.

He asked at both liveries, and no blonde or any other kind of lady, or even gent, had left a thoroughbred in town,

134

either stabled or running loose like a stray cat.

At the depot, it only took a minute to find out nobody had checked a horse of any description aboard an east- or westbound train. The stationmaster asked why a gal running away from an Indian agency for some mysterious reason couldn't just *ride* East. Longarm shook his head and said, "She could, but she never. For one thing, she never went riding that day with saddlebag or a roll on her sidesaddle. For another, we know how often she shopped at the agency trading post and her pantry ain't missing enough grub to matter. Her husband put out an all-points alarm on her even before he noticed the Indian band was also missing. It was while looking for her that the Indian police discovered Raining Stars and his band had ridden off, too. To get anywhere important, starting with just a sissy horse and perhaps some money of her own, the gal would have had to stop for provisions *some* damned place in the Indian Nation. But she hasn't. Nobody from any of the Five Civilized Tribes to the east have seen hide nor hair of any white gal on any kind of mount, let alone a snooty blonde riding a snooty horse sidesaddle. So, alone or in the company of Indians, she could only have ridden west southwest. Since the Cheyenne rode the same way, in what had to be a killing mood, the notion she rode with them willing is sort of loco."

"What if she had an Indian boy friend?"

"It happens. I know for a fact it happens. But we're talking about a snooty gal the Indians didn't like much for some reason. I'll keep that in mind. I keep everything in mind. But all I wanted from you was that she never left from *here* aboard a train."

He went next to the Western Union office. Billy Vail had left a message for him ordering him home. Billy wouldn't get the night letter for a spell, and the office would be closed in the morning, so there was no sense wiring him an argument.

He tried again at the town marshal's office. This time the old man was awake. Some old gents were like that, after nightfall. The town law answered to the name of Shotgun Lew and said he'd heard of Longarm. Longarm said, sure he remembered the time Shotgun Lew had wiped out the Kiowa Nation single-handed, and added, "They tell me at the skating rink they're expecting trouble, Shotgun. Something about company goons busting up the competition. You hear anything about it?"

The old man nodded, spat at a cuspidor near his desk, and missed. "All the time," he said. "Them sassy gals running the summer skating parlor keep asking me for protection. I mean *special* protection, like they was a bank or something. I told 'em they gets the same protection as anyone else here in Fort Reno. No more, no less. It'll be a cold day in the desert when I stations one of my two-only deputies at the door of a durned old skating rink!"

"You mind if I sort of check in on 'em from time to time, Shotgun? It's your town, so it's for you to say."

The old-timer shrugged. "Hell, I don't care. I thanks you for having more manners than some infernal federals, though. This is still my town and, like I told them two young sassy-skirted gals, nobody messes with nobody in Fort Reno if they don't want trouble with *me!* Say, did I ever tell you about the time I shot it out with Santa Anna, personal, back in Thirty-seven or -eight? That's how come he wound up with that wooden laig, see? I nailed that sassy greaser from a mile and a quarter away. I was aiming for his balls, to pay him back for the Alamo, but the wind shifted on me and I only got him in the thighbone. Naturally they had to take his laig off, though. I spits on my rounds afore I loads, and my momma was half rattlesnake."

Longarm nodded soberly, and said, "I've always wondered how that cuss lost that leg, Shotgun. You say you have two deputies to back our play?"

"Yep. I does *most* nights, leastways. Right now Hank Brown's out looking for strays. He raises stock more than he deputies. I disremember where Billy Wort is right now. Ain't seen him in a few days. He's got a gal over to the Red River, and—"

"Never mind," Longarm cut in. "I'll see if anybody ornery-looking gets off the westbound at midnight. Meanwhile I'm sure you'll be able to cover that main street, should the Commanche rise tonight."

Shotgun Lew said, "Damned right, son. Oh, I forgot to tell you I was at Adobe Walls that time Quanna Parker riz."

But Longarm was already leaving. He was too polite to dispute his elders, but it did occur to him that if half the old-timers who'd told him they'd fought at Adobe Walls had been anywhere near the place, Quanna Parker would have been scared to show his face there.

Outside, Fort Reno was looking more trail-town-Saturday-night by the minute as more hands rode in. Since the South Cheyenne Reserve lay on the southwest corner of the Indian Nation, the mostly white range to the south and west produced a mostly white crowd in the town itself. Soldiers on leave from the army post rubbed elbows at every saloon with cowhands, railroad men, and fancy-dressed gamblers. The cowhands, of course, made more noise than anyone else, riding into town. Since word of the jump and massacre had spread considerably, most of the crowd was loaded for bear. If old Shotgun Lew had a town firearms ordinance to enforce, he wasn't enforcing it enough to matter.

But for a change most of the cowhands and cavalry troopers seemed more anxious to fight Indians than one another. It was just as well nobody wearing feathers and paint seemed to enjoy a Saturday night in Fort Reno.

Longarm consulted his watch, saw he had time, and scouted up the only hotel in town. It was next door to the summer skating parlor. So, of course, the night clerk said

137

they had plenty of rooms for hire on *that* side of the second floor. Longarm smiled understandingly and said, "I ain't here to hire a room. I'm a U. S. deputy marshal. I'm here acting nosy. I want you to study hard and tell me if a wispy blonde gal who might or might not have signed in as Helen Hutchins could have stayed here about the time of that reservation jump."

"I don't have to study at all," the night clerk said. "It never happened. That Injun police chief, Whitepony, already asked me the same question nearly a week ago. So I was able to tell him I never seen such a gal here or at any of the parlor houses I visits regular."

Longarm nodded and said, "Whitepony's as smart as he looks. I figured I was sniffing at the wrong lamppost too. But they pay us to ask dumb questions, and I thank you for being so helpful."

"So did Whitepony. What's this all about, Deputy? Do you boys suspicion she run off on her own instead of with them Injuns?"

"Not now. Did Whitepony say why *he* was double-checking?"

"Sure. He said her husband looked like he set down to piss and that it was a well-known fact a frusterpated she-male rode horses a lot, noplace in particular, like their bottoms was itchy. Whitepony said she likely wouldn't have got took had she been home that night, where she belonged, like the other white gals out there."

Longarm shrugged. "He may be right, but she wasn't. Most white folk who get in trouble with Indians are riding where they hadn't ought to be. While I'm here, I'm going next door to watch 'em skate. If someone *did* hire an upstairs room on that side, would they have a line of sight on the proceedings?"

The clerk shook his head and said, "They built that big barn windowless, thank God. There's some vents up by the

138

roof peak, as we know to our sorrow because all the noise comes outten them. But they don't face any of our upstairs windows. Why?"

"Just covering all bets. A gent in my line of work has to. It's been nice jawing with you."

He left and went next door. He found Texas Trixie behind the ticket counter instead of the chubby gent. Two kids dressed cow were fussing at her. Texas Trixie was fussing right back. As Longarm came within earshot he heard one of the young cowhands protest, "It ain't anywheres near midnight, ma'am. And we ain't never been on summer skates yet."

Texas Trixie said, "I know, boys, and I feel for you, but just can't reach you. We're closing early tonight."

"No offense, ma'am, but we hear lots of folk skating inside right now."

"I hear 'em, too. Can't ask 'em to leave till their hour's up. But it wouldn't be fair to take your quarters and make you leave afore you'd spent your full hour on skates. So we ain't selling no more tickets, and that's final."

Longarm joined them as the two young hands started to turn away disgustedly. Longarm said, "Hold it, gents. Miss Trixie, here, ain't thinking as clear as me. Let's see if we can help her change her mind."

Texas Trixie frowned at him and murmured, "Custis, we're trying to empty the place, not fill it up! You remember that midnight train? Well, they're coming. Our barker just gave us the word, before he just quit. Sandy and me aim to padlock the doors before they get here, and we can't hardly do that with a mess of cowboys skating about inside, can we?"

One of the young cowhands asked, "Are you gals in trouble, ma'am?"

She ignored him, but Longarm said, "Boys, a mess of Eastern toughs are on their way here to bust up this here summer skating parlor. So it's only fair to warn you that if you insist on learning to skate tonight, you may wind up in a Dodge City situation."

The two young hands exchanged glances, nodded at each other, and the more talkative one said, "Hot damn. Count us in, pard!"

Longarm grinned at Texas Trixie. "There you go. You haven't been looking at things *clear*, ma'am. How many goons could the skating trust have aboard one old train?"

"Our barker said he got the word there was at least two dozen. That's why he left us so sudden. But are you suggesting the boys here in town would be willing to help us?"

One of the young cowhands said, "Suggest it, hell, ma'am. We'd be proud to kick the never-mind outten any rascals interfering with our skating lessons!" He nudged his sidekick and added, "Ain't that right, Woody?"

Woody nodded and said, "Hell, yes, she's pretty."

Texas Trixie still looked uncertain. Longarm said, "Let 'em in so's they can pass the word, gal. Can't you see it makes more sense to have it out and get it over with than to risk an empty building defending its own self?"

"Of course. But why on earth should the boys here in town fight for Sandy and me?"

"You just heard 'em say you're pretty. These boys have been working all week at a mighty tedious job, and when a cowhand rides into town of a Saturday night, he's *looking* for some action!"

"You must be an old cowhand, mister," said the more talkative one of the pair.

His pal, Woody, said, "Nobody gets to bust up nothing in a cowtown unless the cowboys say he can. How much do a ticket cost, ma'am?"

Texas Trixie laughed. "Go on in, boys. It's on the house."

They both made noises midway between a laugh and a rebel yell and went in swaggering. Texas Trixie asked Longarm, "Could you spread the word, Custis?"

"Don't have to," he told her. "Just started the snowball rolling down the hill. Them two knows the local riders better than me. So they won't invite sissies to the party."

"Oh, wait, some of the townee gals are skating inside tonight. Shouldn't we at least get them out before those thugs show up?"

"Western gals wouldn't miss a show like that for the world. So there's no sense asking 'em to leave. Their escorts will watch out for them."

"What about the soldiers? We have at least a dozen soldiers from the cavalry post inside, and they don't get along too good with the cowboys."

"They will tonight. When it's the neighborhood against outsiders, everybody with hair on his chest pitches in. In a free-for-all, you just punch at any face you ain't seen around town before, see?"

"Had you been here when our barker got that warning wire, he might not have quit, and I could give you some skating lessons instead of being stuck here."

He said, "You was fixing to close, anyway. So why not just leave the door open and let them townees as want to come on in, free?"

"That's a good idea. Most of the skates are hired and we're only losing a dime or so per onlooker, which is a mighty cheap way to hire a private army. Let's go. I'll introduce you to Sandy and the other gals. But remember, I saw you first."

Texas Trixie climbed out from behind her ticket counter with the cash box under one arm and slipped the other arm through Longarm's as they went in together.

As he'd already surmised from the sound outside, the rink was still fairly crowded. There were more townee gals skating, or trying to, than he'd have wanted in the way had he been calling all the shots. But there were at least five

141

gents for every gal and most of the gals looked tough. He knew hired toughs seldom resorted to gunplay; they just busted up a place.

A short plump gal with a handsome set of big brown worried eyes skated over to them and skidded to a graceful stop. Texas Trixie introduced her to Longarm as her business partner, Sandy, and said, "Get him some skates and show him a good time, skating, whilst I put this cash in the safe with the rest. If you two are engaged by the time I get back I'll scratch your eyes out."

She flounced off. Sandy blushed. "Trixie talks fresh, but she doesn't mean it," she told Longarm. "She told me about you, Custis. Circle with me and we'll see about getting you some skates. You do skate, don't you?"

"On *ice,* some. Ain't sure I want to skate on little wheels, even if I can. I mean, I didn't exactly come here to take skating lessons—no offense."

But she was already moving on her side of the guard rail. So he had no choice but to follow on his side until they came to a gap near a bench where another young, pretty gal was in charge of a mess of skates in built-in cubbyholes.

The chubby little blonde skated through the gap to join him and the two of them sat him down. He said, "Hold on, ladies. I hadn't even considered going this far with either of you."

Sandy laughed and said, "We're used to shy customers, Custis. Everybody yearns to skate. What's his size, Mabel?"

Mabel, if that was the brunette's name, said, "Big. But I have a set of Vinelands here that should clamp to those gunboats of his."

She was right. Longarm laughed, feeling silly, as the gal knelt at his feet, putting wheels on them. She keyed the toe clamps to his boots, then fastened the straps across his

142

insteps, fast and professional. "Stand up and try 'em for fit, cowboy."

Sandy warned him, "Let me help you up. Keep your legs together and just relax till you get the feel of it. It's not like ice skates, exactly."

That was for damned sure, he decided, as he got to his feet—or wheels—and would have found himself flat on his ass had not the surprisingly strong little Sandy held his hand, steady as a post. On ice skates a man had to worry about his ankles turning. On rollers his ankles felt fine, but the infernal skates wanted to roll out from under him worse than the blades of sensible winter skates. He grinned sheepishly down at Sandy and said, "Maybe I'd best sit this one out, Sandy. I ain't even been on ice, recent, and this feels just plain ridiculous!"

She insisted, "I can see you have a natural sense of balance. Come on. I won't let you fall. Just stand on them. I'll tow you around the rink a time or two until you get the feel of summer skating."

He didn't have any way of stopping her, it seemed. For, though he planted his feet firmly in place, stubborn as an army mule, he was suddenly out on the floor, being towed like a pull toy by the stubborn little blonde.

He felt about as useless as a pull toy, too, as one of the cowhands he'd talked Texas Trixie into letting in skated past, calling out, "Ride 'em, cowboy!" and then went flat on his ass. It served him right.

Sandy warned, "Don't look back!" as he started to teeter and then recovered his balance, with a lot of help from her.

"Thanks. But is there any point to all this, ma'am?" he asked.

She laughed. "You're doing fine. We'll have you skating on your own in no time. Are you sure you've never done this before?"

"Do I look like a total fool? Look out, we're fixing to run down that couple ahead!"

But they didn't. Sandy swayed them gracefully around the slower pair of townees and as they curved the other way he noticed, to his pleased surprise, that he was helping. He said, "Oh, I get it. It's sort of like winter skating, save that you can't lean your blades—I mean, wheels. You got to sort of bend your ankles to turn. Try that on winter skates and you'll fall down for certain."

She said, "You're not on ice. You're on rock maple. So forget all about skating on ice, damn it. I've found it's usually easier to teach summer skating from scratch. You old ice skaters all seem to start with bad habits I have to break you from. Let's head over there, where the rink's not as crowded."

He had no say in the matter as she towed him into a less crowded corner near the rear of the big barn and said, "Grab the guard rail when you come to it," before letting his hand go unexpectedly.

He moaned, "I'll get you for this!" as he rolled on alone, teetering like a drunk on grease, but somehow managing to stay upright until he crashed into the guard rail and hung on for dear life as his feet rolled on under, out of control. But by the time Sandy joined him there he had the fool rollers under his center of gravity again.

"See? I told you you could skate, Custis," she said.

He laughed. "That was an accident. How do you stop so sudden on them crazy wheels, Sandy?"

She lifted her already sassy skirts to expose a pair of mighty shapely ankles as she showed him how she put one skate crosswise behind the heel of the one she was balanced on.

"Well, that's *something* like stopping on ice skates. But I sure have a lot to learn," he said.

She said, "That's why I'm here. Come on. Just try to

144

relax and we'll circle the rink a few times, easy. Put your arm around my waist, like so."

He did. Her waist felt nice. She wasn't wearing the corset he'd expected, judging by the way her soft curves hourglassed. She put her arm around *his* waist, grabbed one of his hands in her free one, and sort of braced him with her fat little hip as they skated on. He found it easier that way. For one thing, her body pressed against his like that took his mind off falling. He'd forgotten about watching another gal screwing and being chased away from another's bed earlier. But the perfume in her hair sort of reminded him as it drifted up under the brim of his Stetson.

"Try to keep in unison with me, Custis. We're supposed to sway back and forth *together,* see?" she said.

He saw that it was giving him a dawning erection as well as improved balance. But she was likely more used to rubbing butts with total strangers out here in front of everyone. So he stayed polite as, sure enough, they got to skating pretty well together. He asked her where she was from and she said Baltimore. She went on to explain how she'd learned skating as an employee of the established Plimton skating trust but that they were cheap to work for. So, like others, she'd wanted to go into business for herself.

He said, "That sounds fair, even if the Plimton Trust don't seem to like competition. But don't a place like this cost a heap of cash to even start, Sandy?"

"That's for sure. But I'd saved enough to buy the first few Vineland patent skates. Texas Trixie had more, when we joined forces. It was her money that bought this lot and sort of built this building. We still owe the bank for most of it. Between us we could barely scrape up the down payment."

"We'd best make sure nobody burns you out, then. Was Texas Trixie a skating gal, too, before going into business for herself with you?"

145

"Not exactly. She doesn't like to talk much about what she was doing down in Texas before we met here. I think she was an actress or something. But they had a skating rink where she worked in Texas, so once she'd learned to skate good, she said it beat any *other* line of work she'd ever been in. Let's try a waltz."

"Try a *what?*" he gasped, but she was already waltzing him around in circles and, though he was sure he was about to fall, he heard some other gal in the crowd say, "Oh, look, ain't that fancy?" So he just hung on as best he could and took credit for his total confusion being some sort of skater's waltz, wishing it would stop.

As they whirled around and around, he saw Texas Trixie coming their way on her own skates in flashes. Her jaw was set sort of firm as she regarded them. Sandy laughed and said, "Oh, dear, I think she's jealous."

That was the last thing Sandy ever said. For a gun echoed like thunder under the cavernous roof and Sandy just let go of him to fall one way as Longarm, helpless, rolled backwards across the hardwood, fighting for balance and trying to get to his gun. The gun roared again and maple splinters flew up from the part of the floor he'd just rolled over at considerable speed, wondering where the gunfire was coming from and where in the hell he was going.

Others, as confused, either skated out of his path or just dove headlong to the floor as the gun roared a third time. Longarm's heels hit somebody already on the floor and he fell over backwards, firing his own gun at the smoke haze he'd spotted near one of the roof vents above. He crashed to the floor on his back. It hurt. He kept shooting up at the roof vent anyway, until his hammer clicked on an empty chamber.

But it didn't matter. For by now at least a dozen others in the crowd had spotted the same smoke and seemed to be on the same side. They shot all the slats out of the vent in

146

a roaring fusillade that filled the rink with gunsmoke and screams from the gals all around. Longarm knew that anyone still up there was either dead by now or departed for other parts. So he sat up, shucked the fool skates, and jumped up to reload on the run as he made for the entrance, cursing a blue streak.

The street outside was crowded and getting more so as every man in town with ears and a gun came running. Old Shotgun Lew grabbed Longarm by one arm and demanded, "Who's shooting all them guns in my infernal town, God damn it?"

Longarm said, "Bushwhacker, come across the rooftops to fire down into the skating rink from a vent. Let go my arm, damn it. He may still be up there!"

Longarm dashed into the hotel, took the stairs two at a time, and climbed out on the roof, gun in hand. But there was nobody to aim it at. The moon shone down on an open expanse of tarpaper and shingles all around. He could see across to the shot-out vent. There was nobody alive or dead anywhere near it. He cursed and went back down, keeping his .44 out for now, just in case.

In the lobby the night clerk had come out from his cubbyhole to stand there shifting his weight from side to side like a schoolboy trying not to piss his pants. He asked Longarm, "Are you after a gent with a Henry repeater?"

When Longarm said that sounded good enough the night clerk pointed at the front door. "He run out just afore you run in! I don't know how he got in."

"Likely come across the roofs from another direction. What did he look like, pard?"

"Jesus, who *looks* when a man pops outten the stairwell at you with a smoking rifle? I ducked. I didn't consider asking him to hold still and watch the birdie! He was a medium-sized white man with a mighty big gun. After that, all I could swear to was that he was somewhere between

147

sixteen and sixty, and I'd have noticed if he'd been bare-ass or painted blue!"

"God damn it, you have to do better than that! Was he army or cow?"

"Uh, townee, maybe. Wore a suit, not a uniform or chaps, now that I think back. But I can't remember his *hat*, let alone his *face!*"

"How about a moustache? Glasses? *Expression?*"

"I just remember his eyes. No glasses. Eyes, wild as hell. That's when I started ducking. What happened? Who was he shooting at?"

"Me," said Longarm grimly. "The son of a bitch killed another innocent bystander by mistake. This is getting tedious as hell!"

Chapter 10

Texas Trixie had little Sandy's home address, and the local undertaker said he was sure he could get her to keep until they could ship her body home. The skating had, of course, ended for the evening, but as Longarm and Texas Trixie came out of the funeral parlor they were greeted by a lynch mob looking for someone to lynch.

Longarm called out, "Boys, I'm taking Miss Texas Trixie home. Then I'm meeting the midnight train at the depot. Anyone who's in the mood for further exercise can wait for me there and I'll be along directly to explain."

Then he took Texas Trixie by the elbow and led her through the crowd, saying gently, "It's past eleven-thirty, ma'am. I'm sort of confused as to just where your quarters might be. But we want you out of sight before the witching hour."

She said dully, "Sandy and me had a room at the hotel next to the skating rink. Why did he kill her, Custis? She was such an innocent little thing and it hurts so bad."

"I know. I'm pained and I didn't never get to really know her. But the son of a bitch will pay for it. Sorry about my language, ma'am."

"I feel like cussing, too. If I was a man I'd go down to the depot and help you and the others pay him back, too!"

He took her into the hotel. "The man as shot Miss Sandy don't figure to be on that train from the East, Miss Trixie."

149

He snapped his fingers at the clerk and said, "Where's her *key*, damn it?"

The night clerk said, "She's got it. Did you catch that rascal?"

Longarm didn't answer as he took Texas Trixie up the stairs. As she led him down the hall to her quarters she pulled out the key she wore on a string down the front of her bodice. "This is it. Come on in. I ain't in a mood to be alone right now."

"Later, when I bring you good or bad tidings from the depot."

She unlocked the door and stepped inside. He waited until she'd struck a match and lit the oil lamp by the big brass bedstead. Then he said, "Pull your shade and keep away from the window with your shadow, ma'am. When I come back I'll knock twice, then once, then twice again. Don't open your door for anyone else unless you know their voice real well."

She gasped. "Do you think someone could be after *me?*"

"Don't know. It hurts to find such things out the hard way. I'll be back in less than an hour, Lord willing and the creeks don't rise."

He waited until she'd shut the door and bolted it on the inside. Then he nodded grimly and went down and out, to walk the short distance to the railroad depot.

He found the platform crowded with other grim-faced men. He said, "All right, gents, here's the play. I'm a peace officer. So I mean to keep this as peaceable as possible. But we got a tip that some roughnecks are coming to wreck your summer skating rink for a sore loser in court. I'm fixing to ask 'em, polite, to just stay aboard the midnight train and ride on through. Do I have to tell you what to do if they won't listen to reason?"

Old Shotgun Lew crowded forward to say, "Hell, no, Longarm. I just deputized these local boys. So stringing the

150

rascals up will be lawful as well as what they deserve!"

Longarm heard a train whistle to the east. "No stringing without a trial, Shotgun Lew," he told the town marshal. "But tar and feathers ain't a federal offense. Where's the stationmaster?"

The stationmaster shoved close enough to be heard. "Here, getting my ribs crushed. I sure hope you boys can manage this without busting up my station, Deputy!"

"I hope I can. I want you down at the far end, holding the engine, lest I wind up in Amarillo with the bastards by mistake. Can you do it?"

"Sure. I'll watch for you getting on and off. But this is a hell of a way to run a railroad," the stationmaster observed.

"That's all right, pard. Your westbound's running a little fast in any case. For here it comes, and it's only eleven fifty-one."

The train rolled in, with the passengers looking down curiously at the crowded platform. Longarm saw the conductor had only raised the trap above one set of boarding steps, so that was where he headed. He was going up the steps as a burly gent with others crowded behind him was fixing to come down.

Longarm said, "Well, if it ain't old Scars Keller. This is your lucky night, Scars. Recognizing one another from days of yore might save us some tedious discussion. You and your boys can't get off here at Fort Reno, Scars."

The professional tough knew better than to hit Longarm, but he blustered, "Who says so, Longarm? You ain't got nothing on me and mine. I told you the last time we brushed that I'm a licensed private detective."

"That's true, Scars. I know all about your mail-order badge. To save you the bother, I know you know my federal badge don't cut much ice with local matters. But I'm here as a pure and simple Christian, trying to save you from making an awful mistake."

"Since when is getting off a train just to have a drink an awful mistake, Longarm?" Keller asked.

"Since the old town law—who's sort of crazy, by the way—just deputized each and every one of that considerable crowd behind me as a sort of half-official lynch mob. Does that skating trust really pay you goons enough to risk it, Scars?"

"Who said we was working for Plimton Skates?"

"The grapevine, Scars. The boys here in Fort Reno like the brand of skates they just learned to skate on, and they're in an even uglier mood than usual because one of the ladies giving them lessons here has just been murdered. I *told* 'em I didn't think *you* boys done it. But they mostly work cows, so you can figure how many ropes they have handy, can't you, Scars?"

The professional bully blanched. "Hold on now, Longarm! You know I don't *kill* folk for hire!"

"Well, not on purpose, at least. That's why I thought it best to warn you not to get off here. Ain't they got a summer skating rink for you to bust up further west?"

"This was as far west as they sent us, damn it. How am I to justify the expense if we don't get off here?"

"That's your problem, Scars. You can get a train back at Amarillo. I'm sure you'll enjoy Amarillo more than Fort Reno. For one thing, you'll be riding home alive."

"Are you threatening me, Longarm?"

"Nope. Just being neighborly. I don't want to hold this train any longer. So I'm getting off now, Scars. You've a constitutional right to get off with me. But you don't look like a suicidal maniac. So I'd best say adios."

He climbed back down, waved to the stationmaster at the far end, who waved back to the train crew, and the train was shortly on its way again, with Scars Keller and his goons still riding coach.

The Fort Reno boys were disgusted as hell.

• • •

Texas Trixie had trimmed her lamp when he got back to the hotel. Longarm joined her in the darkness and told her it was over for now. She said, "Oh, thank God—and thank *you*, Custis. I don't know what I'd have done without your help. How can I ever repay you?"

"I ain't allowed to collect rewards, ma'am. Poor little Sandy told me you gals had all your savings invested in your rink next door. I'd try to get some sleep now if I was you. What's happened can't be helped. I don't think nothing else *will* happen to you and the other skating gals, now. As for my part in it, your troubles were just a side issue. No offense, but I got other fish to fry. So I'd best get on out to the reservation before the moon goes down."

"Wait!" she pleaded, moving closer. "Can't you stay just a little while, Custis? I'm . . . scared!"

He took her in his arms to comfort her. Then he noticed what she was wearing or, rather, how *little* she was wearing at the moment. "Ma'am, if I don't leave this minute there's no telling how long I might stay. You know how weak-natured us fool men are," he told her.

She reached her bare arms up to pull him down to meet her lips as she sighed. "I'm weak-natured, too," she murmured.

So he kissed her, picked her up, and carried her over to the bedstead without taking his lips from her. She was teasing him, or inviting him, with her passionate tongue as he lowered her to the mattress and started helping her out of her thin chemise. She sighed, "I know how to undress, damn it! Get out of those fool duds of *yours*."

He did as fast as he could, but she'd beaten him by a mile anyway as he mounted her.

Save for her garter belt and black silk stockings, anyway. He didn't mention them until they'd come together once

153

with her long silk-sheathed legs wrapped around his bare waist. Then, as they fell limp together, he kissed her and said, "Howdy, pard. Do you always wear your socks to bed?"

She giggled. "I'd forgotten I had them on. Oh, Custis, I was so afraid you'd go on acting like a gallant fool! Couldn't you tell from the first that I wanted this?"

He moved in her experimentally and said, "Well, as you can likely feel, I was at least mildly interested."

She laughed and moved her hips to meet his teasing thrusts. "If that big tool was any more enthusiastic I'd be in real trouble! God, you fill me nice!"

"You can call me Custis in bed."

She got it, laughed again, and said, "'Fess up, darling. You've been saving that up for a girl just like me, haven't you? I can tell when a man hasn't had a woman in a long time!"

He said, "I don't like to talk about other folk in bed, honey. Why is it you gals always have to ask fool questions like that? Did I just ask you how long it's been since *you've* been laid?"

She sighed and moved her hips faster as she replied, "Too long. Can't you tell?"

He couldn't. No man could *ever* tell. But, what the hell, she wasn't trying to sell him a bill of virginity. And while poor little Sandy had hinted the redhead might have worked at this, down Texas way, in her day, she had to be doing it for pure fun right now, since he hadn't asked or offered money. He'd noticed in the past that a fancy gal making love for purely sentimental reasons did so mighty fancy. So it served Willy May right if he just enjoyed this one instead. He couldn't remember if the nurse screwed this good or not. It seemed the gal one was in at the moment always seemed better than anyone else could be.

For a gal who said she'd invited him to stay because she

was scared, old Texas Trixie sure was brave about *screwing* in the dark, at least. She acted like she couldn't get enough of him and, since he'd been inspired earlier by another gal's bedroom athletics, he kept it up until she finally pleaded for mercy and said, "I'm getting sore as well as sleepy, darling. Can't we save some for the morning?"

He said that sounded fair, and lit a cheroot as she snuggled her red head on his bare shoulder. By the time he'd finished his smoke he found out old Texas Trixie had one fault in bed after all.

She snored. She didn't snore just *annoying*, like most gals. She snored like a bunkhouse full of worn-out cowhands snoring in unison, or a couple of loggers whip-sawing a redwood out California way. He snubbed out the smoked-down cheroot as he considered his options. He was still keyed up because of all the things running around in his brain, chasing their own tails. He was a little ashamed of himself, too. Not for making love to old Trixie, but for wasting so much time on a side issue that had nothing to do with what Billy Vail had sent him down here to look into.

He gently worked his shoulder out from under her red head until, not waking, but disturbed, she rolled over against the wall to lie face down, snoring even louder.

He muttered, "That does it. A man can't hope to get a lick of sleep with a gal who snores in *every* damned position!"

He eased off the bed. She just went on cutting down redwoods as he dressed. He didn't want to leave her behind an unlocked door, so he slid the window sash open and stepped out onto the lower roof next door. It was the one facing away from the skating rink. He studied on that as he closed the sash after him and moved across the tarpaper in the moonlight, trying to figure out how to get down from up here.

155

The answer was a drainpipe running down to the alley behind. He slid down it with no trouble. But that meant anyone climbing the other way, with a Henry repeater, had to have been in good shape. That figured. Most hired guns had to be. It didn't narrow the field enough to matter.

He went to the livery and got his Indian pony. He studied more on the past few hours as he rode back out to the agency. Texas Trixie had thought the man who'd shot Sandy was after her and the other gals. He hadn't told her different, because he already felt bad enough about the son of a bitch blowing away two gals in his immediate vicinity. But despite the switch to a lighter, faster-firing gun, it had to be the same cuss. Scars Keller, for all his faults, wouldn't have been on his way to bust the rink up had the skating trust already sent a hired gun after the competition.

As he topped a rise he saw what looked like sunrise ahead. But it wasn't that late, and the sun hardly ever rose in the north. So it had to be a fire. A big one.

He heeled his stud into a lope. But they still arrived just as the Indians were helping the agency people toss the last water buckets on what was left of the Hutchins house.

He dismounted and ran over to John Miles, standing barefoot in his nightshirt with an empty bucket. He didn't ask what had happened. Any fool could see what had happened. He asked Miles when the fire had started and if anyone was hurt.

Miles said, "Don't know. One of the boys says he heard screaming as the night lit up. But nobody's living in the house."

Whitepony came over to them, holding something that looked like a feather duster in his hand. "Prayer stick," he said. "Old. Made in the Shining Times for good luck, or a curse. It was on the porch. The medicine paint's too charred to tell if the feather tips were blue or white, now."

156

The two white men exchanged glances. Miles nodded and said, "I've heard of hate. But this is just silly! They already got the gal and Hutchins is in the dispensary out of his head. So why burn his house?"

Whitepony held the prayer stick up to the moonlight. "Hear me: I think I see flecks of white among the charred ends. I think someone crazy with hate did this thing!"

Longarm said, "I'd best get over to the dispensary, pronto."

But the Cheyenne said, "I already have men over there on guard. Hutchins and the nurse are safe. Everyone here at the agency knew where they were. They did not attack them. They burned this empty house."

"Yeah, but would someone who ain't *been* on the reservation lately know Hutchins wasn't home?" Longarm asked.

Whitepony nodded soberly. "We will search for sign as soon as it's light enough," he said. "I don't believe in spirits who carry prayer sticks and coal oil, but leave no footprints, do you?"

"Not hardly. What was that about coal oil?"

"You can smell it, closer to the ruins. Somebody poured coal oil on both the front and back porches. Then they lit it. Then they rode or ran away. In the morning we will see which way they went."

Another Indian policeman came over to murmur something in worried Cheyenne to Whitepony. Whitepony said in English, "Shit. Somebody *was* in the house when it burst into flames. We'd better see if we can tell who they were."

They could. The trader brought a lantern from his post as his young wife followed, wrapped in a robe and an innocent expression. He told her to stand back as he handed the lantern to Whitepony. He looked sick as hell himself as Whitepony stepped into the wet black ashes and rolled one

157

of the charred bodies over with his foot. Then he swore. Wetfeather's face hadn't burned beyond recognition, face down.

Whitepony moved over to another, smaller shape. Longarm didn't recognize the features of the dead squaw, but Whitepony grunted and said, "More shit! Pretty Whistle was a wicked young girl. But this was still an ugly way to die. Stupid, too. With a whole reservation to play around on, why did they have to come to this empty house?"

Longarm said, "He was on guard duty. Might have had other reasons for bringing a willing young gal here as well." He was looking at the trader's wide-eyed, innocent wife as he said this, but she never blinked. Some gals were just born actresses.

John Miles said, "Well, they surely picked the wrong time and place to make love. It's sort of obvious one at least of Raining Stars' band come back to finish the Hutchins family right. What in the hell could they have *against* the poor little cuss, Longarm?"

"Don't know. I'd best talk to him some more." Longarm went to the dispensary. Willy May was, of course, as wide awake as anyone would be with a house burning down just a few hundred feet away. She was still wearing her kimono and looking confused. Longarm said, "Knock off the bullshit and wake Hutchins up for me, Willy May. This has got past mysterious into deadly. Have you any strychnine handy?"

"Custis, I just heard," she said. "It was two *other* lovers inside that other house. Can you ever forgive me?"

"No. Wake that asshole up and do it *now*, woman!"

She did, sort of. She gave Hutchins a shot of something less dangerous than strychnine and got out an icepack to rub all over his face until he opened his eyes. Longarm slapped him to make sure they stayed open and said, "All

158

right, sonny. You've had your cry. It's time to start acting like a man."

"Have you found Helen yet?"

"No, they just burnt her picture and your whole house, too. Has it ever occurred to you that you don't get along so good with Indians, Hutchins?"

"I didn't do anything to make them mad at me!" he whimpered.

Longarm slapped him again and said, "Try harder. You admit they didn't seem to like you and your wife. I'll admit you wasn't cheating them. So what's left? Have either you or your woman been screwing around with Indians? I mean all the way, in bed?"

"Oh, my God, what are you suggesting?"

"Ain't suggesting. *Saying*. It ain't supposed to happen, but it happens. I know your wife was pretty, in a frosty, thin-lipped way. So tell me man to man, how many Indian squaws have you ever laid, here or anywhere else?"

"Jesus! None! Never! How could I do such a thing?"

"Easy. The man usually gets on top. All right, let's try it another way. From her picture, your woman don't look too warm-natured, and you, no offense, look like a queer. So if you've never messed with any Indian woman, can you say as much for young good-looking Indian boys, or, hell, while we're at it, ugly Indian men of any description?"

"I'm not a queer! I'm not! I'm not! That time with Billy Perkins wasn't really queer. We were just playing doctor, see?"

"Your mamma catch you often playing doctor? Is that why you married up with another prim-lipped gal who, no offense, looked something like her? I ain't here to make judgements, Hutchins. I'm trying to stop more people from getting killed. So I just don't give a shit about your feelings. I want you to tell me the *truth!*"

Hutchins somehow worked a hand loose and threw the icebag at Longarm, hitting him pretty good, for a sissy.

Longarm felt his swollen lip and said, "Don't do that again. I can see you got a good throwing arm, at least. So mayhaps your mamma was a little hard on you. What about your wife, Helen? Was she a lizzy gal?"

"A *what?*"

"You know, a gal who messed with other gals. I couldn't help noticing you had twin beds. So one of you at least had to be sort of cold-natured for newlyweds. If you ain't queer, was she?"

"God damn you! If I was able to stand up I'd show you whether I was a queer or not! Let me up and I'll clean your plow, you son of a bitch!"

Longarm chuckled. "Damned if you ain't starting to act right again. I figured they was treating you too gentle. I know I'm talking cruel and hurtful, old son, but it's important. So, well, were you and your wife screwing regular or weren't you?"

Hutchins strained hard to break free of his bindings. So hard, in fact, he passed out again. Willy May put a warning hand on Longarm's shoulder and said, "That's enough, Custis. If the Indians don't get him, you will, getting him so excited."

Longarm stood up, rubbing his tongue around inside his lip. "Well, I don't reckon he'd know what his wife was doing behind his back, anyhow. Most men don't. Where'd you get that ice he hit me with, in high summer?"

Willy May said, "From my icebox, of course. We get it fifty pounds at a time from the icehouse in town."

"I'm glad there was only a pound or so in that bag just now. Fifty would have really smarted."

"Do you want to go next door and see if I can kiss it well, darling?"

"I thought you were mad at me, Willy May."

160

"Idiot! I told you I found out who was screwing in that other house all night. Come with me and I'll just *show* you how angry I am, you big goof!"

He rolled his eyes heavenward and muttered, "Why is it, Lord, it never rains but it pours?"

She didn't get it. She wasn't supposed to. He said he had to go scout for sign at daybreak. She said daybreak wouldn't come for hours, but that she'd been wanting to come since he'd arrived. So he just had to go to bed with her and take his beating like a man.

She took his longer-than-usual lopes in her saddle as a compliment and, once he got back into it, he had to admit old Willy May was just as nice between her thicker thighs as the redhead had been between hers. And, even better, Willy May didn't snore at all after he'd screwed her to sleep.

Chapter 11

Scouting for sign by the dawn's early light had been a good idea; the frost on the dry grass made it easier. But it didn't work.

They ignored all the bewildering sign near the agency and circled, mounted, looking for where someone had ridden in or out, lately. There was plenty of sign leading deeper into the reserve, none leading out to the west. Whitepony insisted on sweeping out farther. Longarm and Miles went along with him, even though not even the Indian police riding with them could spy a thing out there on the prairie. One of the Cheyenne said he'd heard the old ones, like Raining Stars, had sometimes wrapped their ponies' hooves in bags of grass. Whitepony told him to shut up.

They scouted out a good five miles before Miles called out, "That's enough, boys. We'd best get the army and them Pawnee. This is going to need professional help."

Whitepony took off his hat and bit it a couple of times before he recovered enough to shout, "What do you call *us*, false Indians? I guess I can track as well as any fucking bald Pawnee! How dare you call me a poor tracker!"

Longarm soothed, "Nobody's saying you can't track, old son. What Johnny means is that there don't seem to *be* no tracks out here. I'd bet money on it. For I got eyes, and I've tracked Modoc over lava beds in my time. They just never come this way."

One of the other Indians grunted. They turned the way

162

he was pointing to see two riders coming toward them from the southwest. Whitepony showed off his eyesight by growling, "Speaking of Pawnee, what could those bald-heads be doing out alone without a keeper?"

The two Pawnee Longarm had met before rode in, singing through their noses in triumph as one held a big floppy trophy aloft. Miles said, "That looks like a saddle they've found. Woman's sidesaddle to boot!"

It was. As the Pawnee joined them, the one with the sidesaddle said, "We found the white woman's horse. We could not bring it back. It's half eaten by the buzzards, ants, and coyotes. Dead at least a week. Down in a draw, half a day's ride southwest. You were right, Longarm. They were making for the Staked Plains. Hear me: by now they have reached them."

"Well, that's a problem for them colored boys of the Tenth Cav to worry about," Miles said. "We got hit closer to home last night, Chief. As you come in, did you notice anyone riding out?"

The Pawnee scout said, "If we had met a strange Indian out there he would be with us right now, alive or dead. We saw nobody else. Just the white woman's horse where Brother Buzzard told us to look for it."

"Could you tell if it was killed, or just abandoned when it couldn't keep up?" Longarm asked.

"It was killed," the Pawnee with the saddle said. "Hit in the head with a war club, more than once. Head bashed in good. Other blows, maybe. Hard to tell, with the hide so chewed up. What does it matter how they killed her horse? Don't you want to know if they killed *her*, too?"

Longarm said, "If she'd been left behind dead, you'd have found her, wouldn't you? If the horse she was riding was killed, that means it was still with them, not run off to die as sissy horses sometimes will on the prairie without attention. You scouted for sign around the dead horse, of course?"

The Pawnee looked at each other sort of sadly. White-pony laughed and jeered. "You *found* no sign! I knew it! No fucking Pawnee born of his father's sister could track a Cheyenne and Raining Stars is still, by Manitou, a Cheyenne!"

"Look, squaw killer, the damned horse had been lying in that draw at least a week," the Pawnee said defensively. "Every damned animal that eats meat had been coming in from all over, messing up any earlier tracks."

"Hah! A coyote's hoofprints look like a pony's? I didn't think a Pawnee could tell one track from another!"

"Hear me, Cheyenne dog-turd sniffer! Brother Wind had been at the dry grass for many days before we got there. The earth is baked hard as your thick skull. If we were Cheyenne we would lie and say we saw pony sign. But we are Pawnee men, not lickspittle Cheyenne who tell the white men what they wish to hear! If you're so good, ride over there and see if *you* can find a hoofprint. We have to get this saddle back to the army post."

John Miles said mildly, "That sidesaddle's the property of my junior agent, boys."

But the Pawnee holding it said, "Fuck you. We work for the army. You are not our agent."

Whitepony smiled eagerly. "Do you want that saddle, boss?" he asked.

But Miles was a *good* Indian agent, so he shook his head. "Let 'em carry it home for now. I'm sure the army will be friendlier about it."

The Pawnee laughed and rode off singing. Neither the whites nor the other Indians could understand the words, but they sure sounded dirty.

Miles let them ride out of rifle range before he spat, shifted in the saddle, and said, "Well, there's no sense in us frying our brains as the sunball rises higher. Let's see if we can get back in time for Sunday dinner, boys."

Willy May and the trader and his wife joined Miles and Longarm in the main quarters. The two gals cooked while the men sat in the parlor, jawing in circles about all the mysterious happenings until Longarm was mighty sick of it. Willy May came in at last to tell them soup was on. She seemed mighty cheerful today, for some reason. The trader's wife acted sort of broody and thoughtful. Longarm didn't ask why.

As they ate, the nurse said she'd sent Hutchins over to the army post, as he'd had a relapse and was *really* out of his head now. Longarm felt his lip and murmured, "Well, he might have got overexcited last night. I know I did. It's likely just as well the B.I.A. will have to send him home to his mamma. They sure picked themselves a winner with that old boy. I wonder why on earth he ever asked to be stationed out here."

John Miles chuckled. "He never. He volunteered for the less wild and woolly Shinnecock Agency just outside New York City. But the job was took and, since he'd been studying Algonquin in preparation to lord it over more domesticated Eastern Indians, they sent him out to help me with the Algonquin-speaking Cheyenne."

He helped himself to another drumstick as he went on. "Some help! Asking him how he managed to get in so bad with the Cheyenne is a waste of time. I don't think the poor kid knows *what* he and his woman done."

The trader said, so innocent he made Longarm sick, *"I've* never had no trouble with South Cheyenne. I've even found they steals less than some. I mind the time I was dealing with Navajo, starting out over to Fort Sumner in New Mexico. Navajo men don't steal at all, but you'd be amazed what their squaws can hide under them big skirts they wears.

165

Caught me a Navajo gal walking out of the trading post with a whole side of bacon clamped betwixt her knees one time."

He caught his young wife's eye and said, "That was long before your time, little darlin', when I was young and handsome."

She smiled back at him so sweetly Longarm had to swallow coffee fast to keep from throwing up.

Willy May brought in the apple pie and cheese. They all settled down to demolish it in silence, like the country folk they were. Later, they went out on the porch to digest in the cooler shade. For a prairie day that had started out with frost on the grass, this particular Sunday afternoon was building up to a scorcher.

The men took off their coats and draped them over the porch rail. But a woman's work was never done, even on a Sunday. The gals went to the kitchen to make some lemonade. They'd just finished and were lugging the bucket out on the porch between them as Miles was saying, "I've been wondering about them tracks we never found this morning, boys. I don't hold with Indians riding on or off a reserve without even bending a grass stem. What if the fire next door was set by a plain old-fashioned murderer?"

The trader's wife gasped and let go her side of the bucket handle. Willy May hung on. So the results were a little messy. The nurse didn't let *all* the lemonade spill, bless her, but Miles laughed and lifted his feet and Longarm sidestepped as a sheet of chopped ice and lemonade spread across the porch planks. The trader's wife sobbed, "Oh, how clumsy of me! I'll get the mop, Willy May."

Miles said, "Let it go, honey. It won't hurt the bare planks and, hot as it is, it'll dry up in no time."

So the gals put the bucket down and served everyone tin cups of lemonade. Longarm took his over to sit on the steps.

Willy May sat down beside him, closer than the occasion might have called for. Miles went on, as if nothing had happened, "Wetfeather did have a way with the ladies. Remember that rifle bullet passing between you and him on the way back from town, Longarm?"

Longarm nodded morosely, staring down at a big chunk of ice that had landed in the dust at the foot of the steps as he resisted the impulse to point out that Wetfeather had been nowhere near when another rifle bullet had shot poor little Funny Eyes out from under him. He was tired of explaining himself to the otherwise charming but suspicious-natured nurse.

Miles took his grudging nod for assent and went on playing range detective. "What if some other otherwise-peaceable gent knowed Wetfeather was using that deserted house as a trysting place? What if he took exception to Wetfeather's wayward ways and saw the chance to put a warm end to the boy's hot nature? Anybody could have had a tin of lamp oil and at least one match."

The trader's wife suddenly ran inside, making odd, stran-gled noises. Miles blinked and asked, "What did I say?"

The trader shrugged. "She's given to sudden starts as don't make much sense to menfolk. Couldn't you find out if that Indian gal he was with had *other* particular admirers, Johnny?"

Miles said that sounded like a good notion indeed. Long-arm didn't like the way they were headed, so he said, "Let's not get the Cheyenne stirred up worse than they already are, gents. We don't know the arsonist knew what particular woman old Wetfeather was in there with at the moment."

He was staring thoughtfully at the trader as he said it, but the son of a bitch was either one hell of a poker player or as innocent as he looked. He said, "That's true. They were likely after that young buck himself. He did have a

167

bold way of looking at women. Even white women. I told him once what would happen if he ever stared at *my* woman that way again!"

Miles asked the nurse, "Did that young rascal ever try to flirt with *you*, Miss Willy May?"

She just giggled. "All men flirt with all women. It's up to the woman to say if it goes any further. Wetfeather was all right, poor thing. I never had any trouble with him."

Longarm wasn't sure of his own poker face right now. He just kept staring at the melting lump of ice, as if it was interesting as hell. And then, as he saw how it was melting and soaking into the dust, it was.

He snapped his fingers. "Son of a bitch! Sorry, Miss Willy May."

They all stared at him in the same curious way. "I had the puzzle put together a couple of ways," he said, "but none of 'em worked, till the last piece just fell into place!"

He rose to his feet, put his frock coat on over his vest and gun rig, and said, "I'll get your hat, inside, too, Johnny. You and me have to ride to town before the three P.M. eastbound can leave."

Miles asked how come, after him, but Longarm just went into the house, grabbed their two Stetsons from the antler rack near the door, and then, since he was already inside, moved out to the kitchen, where the trader's wife sat alone at the table, crying fit to bust.

She looked up, flustered, dabbing at her red face as she murmured something about having a cinder in her eye. Longarm smiled down at her in compassion. "Be still. Ain't got time to talk. Your man didn't do it. Behave yourself in the future lest, next time, you *do* get cinders in your eyes— and everywhere else."

She said she didn't know what he was talking about.

"Sure you do," he said. "Remember, old men have long

168

memories and he knows, now, how to set a love nest on fire, even if he didn't torch your pal himself, *this* time!"

She sure was dumb, for a sneak. She looked as if butter wouldn't melt in her mouth as she asked, "Heavens, whatever are you suggesting?"

"Well, for openers, a divorce would likely be a safer way for you to end it, if you can't behave," he said. "I gotta go, ma'am. You do as you like. But if you can't be good, be *careful* in the future, hear?"

He went back out to find John Miles coated and armed again. They both went across to the police station, saddled a couple of broncs, and rode. Miles was still full of puzzled questions, but it was hard to carry on a conversation with Longarm leading him into town at a steady lope.

As they approached the outskirts of town, Longarm left the wagon trace, calling back, "We'd best circle wide and hit the depot from the other side. Folk watching from a second-story hotel window have a disgusting clear view of the main street, as I found out before, riding out with Wetfeather."

Miles gasped, "Slow down, damn it, and let's discuss what the hell is going *on* here!"

But Longarm led him around the backs of the buildings across the street from the hotel at breakneck speed. Then, as they rode into the shade of the railroad water tower, Longarm reined in. "Nothing's going on yet," he said. "Train ain't due for a good half-hour. We'll tether our mounts here and sort of mosey up the tracks toward the depot."

As they got to the open door of the baggage shed, Longarm told Miles to leave his damn fool coat unbuttoned in case he needed to draw sudden. As Miles did so, the stationmaster came out of the gloom to demand what they were doing there.

Longarm flashed his badge and said, "Stakeout. I want

169

you to go get the town law, quiet, and bring him here. If you mention this to another soul in town your ass will belong to the U. S. government!"

The stationmaster gulped, said he'd ridden for the North in the War, and took off running.

Longarm took out his pocketwatch and said, "We're a mite early. Sorry. It's better to get there too soon than too late."

"Longarm, what in the hell are we here for?" Miles asked.

"Can't tell you yet," Longarm said. "I want you to have an open mind when the folk we may be meeting here show up."

"Who are we talking about? Show up for what, damn it?"

"I said I wanted you to have an open mind, unclouded by my prompting. There's a chance in a million I'm wrong. There's an even better chance they may hope to brazen it through. But that ain't likely. I was set up for a killing last night, more than once, and by now they may have figured out how hard I am to kill. By sheer accident, or a matter of taste, I made a smarter move than I meant to, leaving temporary quarters by way of a window. I'm hoping they think I got so athletic because I was on to them. If I was a killer I was after, and couldn't seem to be able to kill me, I'd get the hell out of town as soon as I could, wouldn't you?"

"That ain't good grammar, but I follow your drift," Miles said. "I don't think I'd wait this long, as a matter of fact."

"Sure you would. There's only one eastbound train running on Sunday. We got here ahead of it. The folk we're waiting on should be here directly, packed, cashed, and sweating ball bearings."

A train whistle howled lonesome way off to the west. They must have been able to hear it in the waiting room as well. For Texas Trixie and the pudgy ticket barker she'd

170

said had quit and left town the night before stepped out on the platform to stare hopefully down the tracks.

Texas Trixie was wearing a travel duster and carrying a carpetbag that thumped like it was filled with chains, or coins, when she set it down. The barker put down another heavy bag and opened his coat to display a plain, businesslike gun rig strapped across him just under his flashy vest.

Longarm nudged Miles and said, "Come on, let's see 'em off." He stepped out into the sunlight with the Indian agent following, still confused.

Texas Trixie looked more sick than confused as she saw what was coming her way. But, like lots of the women he'd been meeting of late, she tried to brazen things out by smiling sweetly and saying, "Why, Custis, imagine meeting *you* here, you naughty thing! You know Mr. Randal, don't you?"

Longarm said, "Yeah. I see he got over his fright and come to save you."

The barker smiled innocently. "That's right. Those goons you sent to Amarillo could be coming back any minute, and it's just not worth it. We paid off the other gals, boxed the skates to be shipped east, and we're giving Fort Reno back to the Indians."

Longarm nodded. "Figured you might. Last night I asked them skating-trust thugs an innocent question and got a funny answer. Scars Keller related to me the astonishing news that there ain't no other skating rinks in these parts. I'd thought there was at least one, not far off, down Texas way."

The barker shook his head and said, "Not that I know of. Don't know of any summer skating parlors in Texas at all. Is that important, Longarm?"

"Not to me. Miss Sandy told me, just before she was shot in the back by a yellow-livered polecat, that Miss

171

Trixie, here, learned to skate in Texas. That was why they called her Texas Trixie."

The redhead looked abashed, recovered, and said, "Oh, I know how poor Sandy got that notion. I *am* from Texas. But I learned to skate back East when I was visiting relations in Ohio."

She shouldn't have mentioned Ohio. John Miles had been studying the face under the red hair all this time, of course. So, when she mentioned the part of the country Helen Hutchins had hailed from in the first place, Miles gasped and said, "By Jesus, you *are* Helen Hutchins, with your hair dyed fire engine and your face painted scandalous!"

After that things started happening even faster than Longarm had anticipated. The cowardly barker, Randal, ducked behind Texas Trixie—or Helen Hutchins—as he slapped leather. Longarm, of course, beat him to the draw, but with a lady who screwed so good between his .44 and its intended target he hesitated just long enough for Randal to shove the fake redhead headfirst at Longarm as he crawfished backwards through the depot door.

Longarm sidestepped to let the treacherous she-male sprawl face down on the platform between him and Miles. They didn't owe her a more graceful landing. It was just as well he'd let her fall, when Randal plowed the air where she and Longarm would have been, had he caught her as expected, with a round of .44-40.

Longarm returned the compliment with a potshot into the dark waiting room and, without waiting for results, snapped, "Sit on her, Johnny!" and dashed after Randal. The waiting room was empty save for gunsmoke. But as Longarm ran for the far entrance, facing the main drag, another gun went off, louder than any .44-40. Longarm crabbed to one side to peer out a window by the door as he reconsidered his options.

The pudgy barker lay spread-eagled in the dusty street

172

with his face blown off. Shotgun Lew, the old town law, was standing over him with a smoking twelve-gauge. Longarm was reloading his .44 as he stepped out to join them. The old-timer said, "How do, Sonny. Is this the rascal the baggage boy said you was after?"

Longarm nodded soberly. "Yep, lucky for all concerned. Don't you ever ask questions, old-timer?"

"Shoot, boy, how did you think I got to *be* an old-timer? When I'm on the prod it ain't advisable to come running my way gun in hand unless I knows you mighty personal. Who *was* this silly son of a bitch, anyhow?"

"Used to work over to the summer skating parlor. *Said* he just worked there, anyhow. It's starting to look like he was a silent partner, hiding behind women's skirts from the skating trust. He'll keep a minute. Come on, Shotgun Lew, I got another prisoner for you."

"Hot damn! You mean *I* gets to keep him? I thought you was federal, Longarm!"

"I am. But being a murder accomplice to local murder ain't federal. The gent you just gunned committed arson as well as murder on federal property last night, but I sure don't have no use for the son of a bitch in his present condition."

A couple of townees had come curiously to within conversing distance by now, so Shotgun Lew said, "Boys, make sure this gent don't get away till I get back," as he stepped over the corpse to follow Longarm into and through the depot.

On the platform, John Miles wasn't really sitting on Helen Hutchins. But he had her still sitting on the splinters, crying, as he held up a little .32 whore pistol. "She had this under her garter. Ain't that a bitch?" he said.

The redhead saw the old town law and wailed, "He trifled with my person, and I want you to arrest him for attempted rape, Marshal!"

173

Shotgun Lew aimed the muzzle of his shotgun thoughtfully at Miles. But Longarm told him not to be silly and added, "He's on our side. This triple-crossing treacherous *she-male* gets to admire the interior of your jail till the circuit judge can get around to hanging her."

The gal bawled, "Oh, no, you *can't*, Custis! Not after all we've meant to each other, darling!"

"What you meant to me was an easy woman, and I ought to be ashamed of myself. What I meant to you was another man you could trick and, had not you fell asleep and snored after such an exciteful evening, your true love might have got to gun me with my pants down literal, you sassy bitch!"

Shotgun Lew looked puzzled. "Is that all we got to hang her for? Simple fornication with murderous intent, sonny?"

Longarm grinned sheepishly. "No. Like I said, I was just being young and foolish." His face hardened as he added, "Last night, as she pretended to be putting cash in the safe while I skated with an innocent young gal they thought no more of than a rat in a barn, she ducked into the hotel next door, alerted that gent you just shot to a mighty tempting target, and then got back, looking innocent, just as he crept across the rooftops to blow me away with a rifle. You'll likely find two rifles, a Henry repeater and a .50 Express, among the skating supplies they're shipping east, or intended to. When they shot little Sandy instead of me, she tried to set me up again, Samson and Delilah style. As you can tell by the way I'm still standing here, it didn't work. She must have been the brains. When she woke up, likely as I'd just stepped out her window, she ran to where her confederate was waiting, told him to ride on ahead and see if he could ambush me by moonlight, and, while he was at it, burn down her old quarters at the agency in case she hadn't stripped it of evidence total. He missed me, or chickened out, on the trail. But he found a tin of coal oil on the back porch and set fire to the house, not knowing,

174

or caring, that an Indian couple was using it at the time to play slap-and-tickle."

Miles cut in to say in a confused tone, "Hold on, Longarm. What about that Indian prayer stick Whitepony found amid the ruins?"

Longarm shrugged. "We can't ask Randall now, if he did that to throw more suspicion on the Indians, or if one of your Cheyenne tossed it at the fire to put it out, then just kept quiet. Folk don't boast on prayers that don't work. Any damned body can throw an old feather duster at anything, Johnny. I thought for a time it could have been the trader. But it wasn't. So forget it."

"Why in the hell would the trader want to do a thing like that, Longarm?"

"He didn't. That's why we can forget it. The killings and arson out there has been paid for. Shotgun Lew, do you have a pair of handcuffs, or would you like to borrow mine?"

The old-timer produced a set of cuffs and said, "Hold out your hands, ma'am, and I'll get you outten this hot sun. You'll like our jail. We serves white bread and beans twice a day, whether you're hungry or not. Behave yourself, and you'll get salt on your beans."

She did no such thing. So Miles hauled her to her feet and Shotgun Lew cuffed her wrists behind her to teach her not to try to hide them like that from the law. Longarm said, "Let's go. It's a quiet Sunday afternoon, but the streets will still be crowding up if we don't get cracking."

He was right. A considerable crowd of townees had gathered to watch the entertainment as they frog-marched Helen Hutchins the short way to jail, her head held defiant.

Miles, walking beside her, asked, "How come you run off and colored your hair so crazy, Miss Helen? We all thought the Indians had kidnapped you!"

"Oh, shut up, you old fool!" she said.

Longarm told Miles, "That part was luck. She just rode to the edge of town, dismounted, and left her thoroughbred to wander home or anywhere it wanted. Then she changed her appearance and joined the summer skating bunch she already knew, with the money they needed to finish setting up. Poor little Sandy must have noticed how her hair had found its way from dishwater blonde to red, sudden, but women don't mention secrets like that about one another and Sandy really thought she was Texas Trixie, like she said. Sandy, of course, had never been anywheres near the Indian agency."

Miles asked, "How did you figure it out, Longarm? Oh, wait, right—you seen the picture of her out at the Hutchins house."

"Wrong. That's why she sent Randal to burn the place, and the pictures I'd seen, once they felt I was breathing down their necks, smarter than most. She never *left* no tintype of her own self on her husband's desk. What gal running off would have? I seen two. One young battleaxe, who wasn't her and another picture of an *older* battleaxe with what I thought was just a mild resemblance. I should have looked closer by candlelight. But I can still picture both pictures in my head. So they had to be two different tintypes of the *same gal*, took brideful and middle-aged. Poor young Hutchins was mighty attached to his mean-faced mother, which was probably one good reason to run off. The other, of course, was that Helen had married him hoping to be posted near New York City, not way out here in a place even more country than Ohio. Ain't that right, Miss Helen?"

By then they'd reached the jail. Miles and Longarm let the old-timer have the fun of booking her and locking her away. Longarm said Shotgun Lew would find them over at the saloon across the street when he felt like it.

Suiting deeds to words, they crossed over, took a corner

table, and ordered needled beer. As Longarm lit a cheroot, Miles said, "I'm still missing some things about her as well as a bunch of Indians, pard. You said she run off with a mess of money. Where'd she get it? I know how much they pay a junior agent, for I used to be one. I told you I went over the books, too. Had she saved it from back home?"

Longarm shook out his match and said, "Not hardly. She must have been dirt poor and anxious to improve herself when she married up with a mamma's boy who preferred twin beds. I know a man ain't supposed to talk about such matters behind a lady's back, Johnny, but you have my word that gal enjoyed old-fashioned loving more than most. She married Hutchins hoping for a more glamorous life. You live out here, so we'll say no more about how exciting she must have found it. But she couldn't run off as broke as he'd found her. So she started putting away nuts for the winter or, in this case, summer. Knowing you were on your way back to the agency, and knowing you had to be smarter than her husband, she ran off with her ill-gotten gains just before you could get there and catch her."

"Catch her doing *what*, damn it? I told you the books don't show any real money lost, strayed, or stolen!"

"That's 'cause she was helping her weak husband keep 'em. She was too slick to tack on nonexistent wards of the government. She just never had to pay out cash to any as *didn't come in* once a month for it, for almost half a year. No one Indian gets all that much. But it can add up handsome when you're talking about fourteen or fifteen families, and anybody can draw an X or a scribbled arrowhead on the pay book. *He* never noticed, as he handled the heavier rations with the help of Indians he was scared skinny of. Helen did give cash to most of the family heads who came to the table. It was easy for her just to sign an extra X now and again when he wasn't looking and slip the cash away for *herself!*"

The waitress brought their drinks. She wouldn't have been worth looking at even if Miles hadn't been so puzzled. "That's an old dodge," he said. "But it don't work good, as many a crooked agent has discovered the first time his books got audited. You can't just *make up* Indians, Longarm. Each one has a name and number on file."

Longarm said, "Sure," took a sip from his schooner, and put it back down to explain. "Old Raining Stars and his band were the only ones she needed. They was mostly old, and the doc says they had fever in their camp. You know they was stubborn, proud, living way off by themselves in piss-poor shelter, awful sanitation, almost invisible. You know last winter was a rough one. So they started dying. They didn't die off sensible, like the B.I.A. regulations say they have to. As each old-time Crooked Lancer gave up the ghost the others just carried him, or her, over to the treetop unofficial medicine ground and stuck 'em up in the sky. The wolf wind and ravens soon reduced 'em to scraps, and who can read names off tombstones that don't exist? As survivors came in for their money and supplies, they would have reported at the more important money table that, say, One Sock In The Wash or Big Chief Tom-Tom wasn't there because he was dead. Raining Stars was sullen but honest, as I recall. But all the gal had to do was thank 'em for the information and sign the dead for the usual anyways. She was keeping the ledger. Hutchins was just passing out the grub, see?"

Miles frowned and said, "Jesus, that not only works, I'm ashamed of myself for never having thought of it! But the whole band couldn't have died off so convenient for her, Longarm!"

"Why not? One or two at a time, at least. The trader says he wasn't selling the band hardly anything most of the winter. When I scouted out there for sign the camp had been salvaged by others who may see no need to report

178

petty theft to the B.I.A., and nobody *else* had been shitting in the willows much. The last to die would have been the stronger left. They put *most* of the bodies out in the cotton-woods to get blowed away in the wind. Near the end, those still left must have been mighty moody. When a Plains Indian figures he's about to die, and there's nobody around to keen over him, he just wanders off, like they say elephants do. Who's going to notice a sick old Indian singing to himself under a cottonwood on medicine ground the others avoid when it ain't important? Who's to say whether a pile of bones and rags fell out of a tree, or just died there, alone, unceremonious?"

Miles nodded and said, "I can follow that so far, but no further. I can see how, noticing a white gal was missing and paying more attention to business, my police could have noticed nobody was at Raining Stars' camp, either, and added two and two to get six or seven. If they never jumped at all, that sure explains why nobody could track 'em. But have you forgotten them murdered cowhands, and the way Miss Helen's horse wound up clubbed to death on the prai-rie, not home?"

Longarm took another swig of needled beer. "That was what was mixing me up. The other parts fit easy, till one had to consider stock and other critters killed Indian style when no other Indians could have done it. It came to me watching lemonade ice melt, out at your place, just now."

"I recall the accident, Longarm. But if you try to tell me lemonade's a deadly weapon, I'll have to call you a lunatic!"

Longarm chuckled. "My boss calls me that all the time. This time I get to tell Billy Vail he sent me down here on a wild goose chase. Though, come to think on it, it's a good thing he did. Remember that gullywashing storm we had, just about the time Miss Helen decided to be Texas Trixie?"

"Sure. It was a humdinger. So what?"

"So it wasn't raining lemonade or even stars that night.

179

But just about the time she was dyeing her hair at the hotel it was raining fire, salt, and *hail!* You ever notice how big summer hailstones can get, Johnny?"

Miles nodded, started to ask another dumb question, then said, "Thunderation! Of course! Most hail just comes down pea-sized and stingful, but here and there a patch of ice balls the size of onions come down hard enough to smash through a barn roof!"

"Or a skull," Longarm said. "Them drovers was camped dumb, in a draw. Her horse was just born dumb, like most thoroughbreds, so after it strayed it took shelter out of the wind, too, as hail balls big and hard as bricks come down, bouncing off the sides of them two draws to sort of focus on anyone or anything with its head in the way. Hail just hitting soft parts would have only left bruises nobody would notice, once said flesh spoiled some. But a skull bone dimpled in by a hailstone hitting big and solid as rock would have left a wound just like a stone-headed war club makes. The rain with the hail moved the bodies about, spreading 'em out like they'd been in a running fight. Stock on higher ground and tougher mostly lived. Some got 'butchered' by coyotes. Then the sun come out to dry everything out, melt the hail, and leave sign nobody could read sensible."

Miles said, "I'll be a son of a bitch! It's all so simple, once you show the way. I reckon you think I'm dumb as hell, don't you?"

Longarm shook his head. "Nope. I'm just *smart* as hell. At least, I am today. Until I studied that melting ice I just couldn't make it fit together any better than you could. I'd thought the missing gal might be playing purloined letter, since if she hadn't been carried off by Indians and hadn't left the area any other way, she had to be *some* damned place. I would have suspected the so-called Texas Trixie sooner had I not been too dumb to ask Hutchins how many pictures of his mamma he had when he said there were

180

pictures of his mamma and his wife on his desk. Poor little Sandy was blonde, but of course she didn't look nothing like the picture I had in my head of Helen Hutchins. Texas Trixie came closer to the description you all gave me, aside from the hair, which I knew right off was not her natural color. But her face wouldn't fit anything I'd seen framed. So I couldn't figure out what on earth she was up to, even when it started to look like she had to be up to *some* damned something."

He swallowed more needled beer and continued, "You'd have caught her without my help, had not that unexpected hailstorm covered her tracks with confusion she never planned. She left so sudden because she feared a man like you who knew his business would get around, sooner or later, to wondering why Raining Stars' band never came in no more, even though the books said they had to be somewhere closer than up a tree. She hoped to play another gal entire, in front of everyone, acting less sedate. But I reckon if you hadn't jumped to conclusions about that reservation jump, somebody taking skating lessons would have caught on soon enough. She was more lucky than smart. She couldn't have expected her husband to go crazy with grief and such. But by the light of the recent cold gray dawn, she and her boy friend had to have figured they were pressing their luck past reason. So you know the rest.

"Maybe if we send word to Hutchins at the army hospital he'll snap out of it. I think he's more upset by the notion of a gal he hardly ever touched being touched by a mess of redskins than he is by her just being missing. Even sleeping in twin beds, I don't envy him her *snoring!*"

Miles said, "I'll have to send word to the army, of course. Want to tell Whitepony and my boys all about it first. They deserve a laugh at the expense of them sassy Pawnee. Maybe I'll get around to it tomorrow. Hutchins is through as an Indian agent, whether he gets better or not. Anyone can crack up. But, damn it, he was supposed to watch the store whilst I was away!"

Shotgun Lew came in, sat down, and said, "She sure does scream a lot, considering the circuit judge can't possibly hang her in less'n a good two weeks or more. What are you boys drinking? It sure looks coolsome."

Longarm ordered another round but didn't see fit to repeat himself to the old-timer, who had all he needed to hold the treacherous bitch in any case. Then he took out his watch and said, "Well, the one and only westbound today is due in about an hour. That just gives me time to check my saddle and possibles with that friendly stationmaster. Can you get my Indian pony back home, Johnny?"

Miles nodded but said, "You got plenty of time and it's hot as the hinges of hell out there this afternoon. I still owes you two drinks, Longarm."

That sounded fair. But half an hour later Longarm got up, shook hands all around, and headed for the depot. He took the saddle and possibles off the pony still tethered under the water tower to the baggage shed. The stationmaster said he'd be proud to see the gear got to Denver sooner or later. So Longarm moseyed to the waiting room, wondering why he hadn't stayed for at least one more drink with the boys.

The scent of gunsmoke had cleared away, but it was still hot and stuffy in there. He stepped out on the platform to wait. A young gal was sitting on her Saratoga trunk, looking mournful. He walked over to her, ticked the brim of his Stetson, and said, "I can check that trunk through for you, ma'am. No offense, but you don't look powerful enough to carry it aboard the westbound."

She looked up sort of sadly and said, "I'm not waiting for the westbound, Deputy Long. I have to head back *east,* I guess, now."

He studied her closer. Her hair was light brown, pinned up under her picture hat. Her face was pretty. Her big hazel eyes were more so, sad as they were. He smiled down at her and asked, "Do I know you, Miss..."

"Cynthia. Cynthia Dormer. I was working at the summer skating parlor last night. Got fired this morning. I guess you don't remember me, huh?"

"Sure I do," he lied, adding, "you skate real fine. But, as you may recall, I was busy dodging bullets. I hope they paid you what you had coming."

"Texas Trixie's been arrested," she confided. "I just heard about it. But she did give me *half* my back wages. Said she'd send me and the other girls the rest later. That's how come I got to go home."

He sighed. "I hate to be the one to tell you this, Miss Cynthia, but what you got from that sneaky she-male is all you'll ever see. They got her for abetting in the murder of your pal, Sandy. If she's got any money at all, she'll surely need it for her lawyer. She's going to need a *good* one."

Far across the prairie to the east a train whistle sounded almost as mournful as she did, as she said, "Oh, my God! What happened! You have to tell me all about it!"

He said, "There's hardly time, if that's the westbound I just heard. But you'll be able to hear all about it long before any eastbound stops here, Miss Cindy. You see, the eastbound ain't coming no more today. Next one's due about nine tomorrow morning."

"Are you sure? I checked out of the hotel! The clerk said I could buy my ticket once I got aboard, and—"

"Miss Cindy," he cut in, "that half-blind clerk at the hotel hardly ever gives straight answers. You should have heard him describe a hotel guest as a total wild-eyed stranger last night. I'm sorry, but there just ain't no eastbound train this afternoon."

She looked like she was fixing to burst out crying, so he said, "Look, I know what you think of Fort Reno, even when you got a job. Do you really have to go east at all?

183

It's a pure waste of time if you only mean to pick up mail there."

"Oh, dear, I don't know *where* I want to go now. You have me so confused about Sandy and Texas Trixie and trains and all!"

He said, "Well, why don't you board the westbound with me, then? I'll see to your trunk. I'm strong as anything. Then we can talk about what happened here, and by the time we get to Amarillo you can make up your mind if you want to get off there or go on to Denver. I know it sounds like bragging, but Denver is the only place around here worth going."

She frowned and said, "I've never been to Denver, but I hear it's nice. Do you think a girl like me could get another job there?"

"I'd say a girl like you could get a job most anyplace, Miss Cindy. But it's easier by far in a big town like Denver."

She didn't answer. He knew better than to press her as she thought as hard as she could. She didn't look like a fast thinker. Gals that pretty seldom had to be.

But the train settled it, rolling in from the east. She stood up and said, "I surely don't want to spend the night just sitting *here!*"

So he whistled, hard, and when the stationmaster stuck his head out, called, "Get this trunk aboard, checked through to Denver, will you?"

As the station hand came over to pick up the Saratoga trunk, sort of grinning, Cynthia Dormer looked confused and said, "Wait, I'm not sure how far I'll be going with you, Deputy Long!"

He just smiled and said, "My friends call me Custis. We can talk aboard the train about how far you want to go with me, honey."

45

LONGARM

Explore the exciting Old West with one of the men who made it wild!